MURDER AT CHRISTMAS

MURDER AT CHRISTMAS

Ten Classic Crime Stories for the Festive Season

Selected by Cecily Gayford

Margery Allingham · Ellis Peters
Edmund Crispin · John Mortimer
Nicholas Blake · Michael Innes
Gillian Linscott · Ethel Lina White
Julian Symons · Dorothy L. Sayers

P

PROFILE BOOKS

First published in Great Britain in 2019 by
PROFILE BOOKS LTD
3 Holford Yard
Bevin Way
London WC1X 7JQ
www.profilebooks.com

1 3 5 7 9 10 8 6 4 2

Typeset in Fournier by MacGuru Ltd
Printed and bound in Great Britain by CPI Group (UK) Ltd, Croydon CR0 4YY

A CIP catalogue record for this book is available from the British Library.

ISBN 978 1 78816 339 2
eISBN 978 1 78283 607 0
Book Club edn ISBN 978 1 78816 468 9

Contents

The Snapdragon
and the C.I.D.

Margery Allingham

'Murder under the mistletoe – and the man who must have done it couldn't have done it. That's my Christmas and I don't feel merry, thank you very much all the same.' Superintendent Stanislaus Oates favoured his old friend Mr Albert Campion with a pained smile and sat down in the chair indicated.

It was the afternoon of Christmas Day and Mr Campion, only a trifle more owlish than usual behind his horn-rims, had been fetched down from the children's party which he was attending at his brother-in-law's house in Knightsbridge to meet the Superintendent, who had moved heaven and earth to find him.

'What do you want?' Mr Campion inquired facetiously. 'A little pocket conjuring?'

'I don't care if you do it swinging from a trapeze. I just want a reasonable explanation.' Oates was rattled. His dyspeptic face with the perpetually sad expression was slightly flushed and not with festivity. He plunged into his story.

'About eleven last night a crook called Sampson was found shot dead in the back of a car in a garage under a small drinking club in Alcatraz Mews, named the Humdinger. A large bunch of mistletoe which had been lying on the front seat ready to be driven home, had been placed on top of the body partially hiding it – which was why it hadn't been found before. The gun, fitted with a silencer, but wiped of prints, was found under the front seat. The dead man was recognised at once by the owner of the car, who is also the owner of the club. He was her current boyfriend. She is quite a well-known West End character called "Girlski". What did you say?'

'I said "Oe-er",' murmured Mr Campion. 'One of the Eumenides, no doubt?'

'No.' Oates spoke innocently. 'She's not a Greek. Don't worry about her. Just keep your mind on the facts. She knows, as we do, that the only person who wanted to kill Sampson is a nasty little snake called Krait. He has been out of circulation for the best of reasons. Sampson turned Queen's evidence against him in a matter concerning a conspiracy to rob Her Majesty's mails, and when he was released last Tuesday he came out breathing retribution.'

'Not the Christmas spirit,' said Mr Campion inanely.

'That is exactly what *we* thought,' Oates agreed. 'So about five o'clock yesterday afternoon two of our chaps, hearing that he was at the Humdinger, where he might have been

2

expected to make trouble, dropped along there and brought him in "to help our inquiries" and he's been in ever since. Well, now. We have at least a dozen reasonably sober witnesses to prove that Krait did not meet Sampson at the club. Sampson had been there earlier in the afternoon but he left about a quarter to four saying he'd got to do some shopping but promising to return. Fifteen minutes or so later Krait came in and stayed there in full view of Girlski and the customers until our ministering angels turned up and collected him. Now what do you say?'

'Too easy.' Mr Campion was suspicious. 'Krait killed Sampson just before he came in himself. The two met in the dusk outside the club. Krait forced Sampson into the garage and possibly into the car and shot him out of hand. With the way the traffic has been lately he'd hardly have attracted attention had he used a mortar let alone a gun with a silencer. He wiped the weapon, chucked it in the car, threw the mistletoe over the corpse and went up to Girlski and the rest to renew old acquaintance and establish an alibi. Your chaps, arriving when they did, must have appeared welcome.'

Oates nodded. 'We thought that. That *is* what happened. That is why this morning's development has set me gibbering. We have now two unimpeachable witnesses who swear that the dead man was in Chipperwood West at six last evening delivering some Christmas purchases he had made on behalf of a neighbour. That is a whole hour after Krait was put under arrest. The assumption is that Sampson returned to Alcatraz Mews some time later in the evening and was killed by someone else – which I do not believe. Unfortunately the Chipperwood West witnesses are not the kind of people we are going to shake. One of them is a friend of yours. She asked our Inspector if he knew you because you were "so good at crime and all that nonsense".'

'Good Heavens!' Mr Campion spoke piously as the explanation of the Superintendent's unlikely visitation was made plain to him. 'I don't think I know Chipperwood West.'

'It's a suburb which is becoming fashionable. Have you ever heard of Lady Larradine?'

'Old Lady 'ell?' Mr Campion let the joke of his salad days escape without being noticed by either of them. 'I don't believe it. She must be dead by this time!'

'There's a type of woman who never dies before you do,' said Oates with apparent sincerity. 'She's quite a dragon I understand from our Inspector. However, she isn't the actual witness. There are two of them. Brigadier Brose is one. Ever heard of him?'

'I don't think I have.'

'My information is that you'd remember him if you'd met him. We'll find out. I'm taking you with me, Campion. I hope you don't mind?'

'My sister will hate it. I'm due to be Father Christmas in about an hour.'

'I can't help that.' Oates was adamant. 'If a bunch of silly crooks want to get spiteful at the festive season someone must do the homework. Come and play Father Christmas with me. It's your last chance. I'm retiring in the summer.'

He continued in the same vein as they sat in the back of a police car threading their way through the deserted Christmas streets, where the lamps were growing bright in the dusk.

'I've had bad luck lately,' he said seriously. 'Too much. It won't help my memoirs if I go out in a blaze of no-enthusiasm.'

'You're thinking of the Phaeton robbery,' Mr Campion suggested. 'What are you calling the memoirs? *Man-Eaters of the Yard?*'

Oates's mild old eyes brightened, but not greatly. 'Something of the kind,' he admitted. 'But no one could be blamed for not solving that blessed Phaeton business. Everyone concerned was bonkers. A silly old musical star, for thirty years the widow of an eccentric Duke, steps out into her London garden one autumn morning leaving the street door wide open and all her most valuable jewellery, collected from strongrooms all over the country, lying in a brown paper parcel on her bureau in the first room off the hall. Her excuse was that she was just going to take it to the Bond Street auctioneers and was carrying it herself for safety! The thief was equally mental to lift it.'

'It wasn't saleable?'

'Saleable! It couldn't even be broken up. The stuff is just about as well known as the Crown Jewels. Great big enamels which the old Duke had collected at great expense. No fence would stay in the same room with them, yet, of course, they are worth the earth, as every newspaper has told us at length ever since they were pinched!'

'He didn't get anything else either, did he?'

'He was a madman.' Oates dismissed him with contempt. 'All he gained was the old lady's housekeeping money for a couple of months which was in her handbag – about a hundred and fifty quid – and the other two items which were on the same shelf, a soapstone monkey and a plated paper-knife. He simply wandered in, took the first things he happened to see and wandered out again. Any sneak thief, tramp or casual snapper-upper could have done it, and who gets blamed? Me!'

He looked so woebegone that Mr Campion changed the subject hastily. 'Where are we going?' he inquired. 'To call on her ladyship? Do I understand that at the age of one hundred and forty-six or whatever it is she is cohabiting with a Brig? Which war?'

'I can't tell you,' Oates was literal as usual. 'It could be the South African. They're all in a nice residential hotel. It's the sort of place that is very popular with the older members of the landed gentry just now.'

'When you say "landed" you mean as in Fish?'

'Roughly, yes. Elderly people, living on capital. About forty of them. This place used to be called "The Haven" and has now been taken over by two ex-society widows and renamed "The Ccraven" with two Cs. It's a select hotel-cum-Old-Ducks' Home for "Mother's Friends". You know the sort of place?'

'I can envisage it. Don't say your murdered chum from the Humdinger lived there too?'

'No, he lived in a more modest outfit whose garden backs on to the Ccraven's grounds. The Brigadier and one of the other residents, a Mr Charlie Taunton, who has become a bosom friend of his, were in the habit of talking to Sampson over the wall. Taunton is a lazy man who seldom goes out and has little money but he very much wanted to get some gifts for his fellow guests – something in the nature of little jokes from the chain stores, I understand – but he dreaded the exertion of shopping for them and Sampson appears to have offered to get him some little items wholesale and to deliver them by six o'clock on Christmas Eve in time for him to package them up and hand them to Lady Larradine, who was dressing the tree at seven.'

'And you say that Sampson actually did this?' Mr Campion sounded bewildered.

'Both old gentlemen swear to it. They insist they went down to the wall at six and Sampson handed the parcel over as arranged. My Inspector is an experienced man and he doesn't think we shall shake either of them.'

'That leaves Krait with a complete alibi. How did these Chipperwood witnesses hear of Sampson's death?'

'Routine. The local police called at Sampson's home address this morning to report the death only to discover the place closed. The landlady and her family are away for the holiday and Sampson himself was due to spend it with Girlski. The police stamped about a bit no doubt, making sure of all this, and in the course of their investigations they were seen and hailed by the two old boys in the other garden. The two were shocked to hear that their kind acquaintance was dead and volunteered the information that he was with them at six.'

Mr Campion looked blank. 'Perhaps they don't keep the same hours as anybody else,' he suggested. 'Old people can be highly eccentric.'

Oates shook his head. 'We thought of that. My Inspector, who came down the moment the local police reported, insists that they are perfectly normal and quite positive. Moreover, they had the purchases. He saw the packages already on the tree. Lady Larradine pointed them out to him when she asked after you. She'll be delighted to see you, Campion.'

'I can hardly wait!'

'You don't have to,' said Oates grimly as they pulled up before a huge Edwardian villa. 'It's all yours.'

'My dear boy! You haven't aged any more than I have!' Lady Larradine's tremendous voice, one of her chief terrors as he recollected, echoed over the crowded first-floor room where she received them. There she stood in an outmoded but glittering evening gown looking as always, exactly like a spray-flecked seal. 'I knew you'd come,' she bellowed. 'As soon as you got my oblique little SOS. How do you like our little hideout? Isn't it *fun*! Moira Spryg-Fysher and Janice Poole-Poole wanted something to do so we all put our pennies in it and here we are!'

'Almost too marvellous,' murmured Mr Campion in all sincerity. 'We really want a word with Brigadier Brose and Mr Taunton.'

'Of course you do and so you shall! We're all waiting for the Christmas tree. Everybody will be there for that in about ten minutes in the drawing-room. My dear, when we came they were calling it the Residents' Lounge!'

Superintendent Oates remained grave. He was startled to discover that the Dragon was not only fierce but also wily. The news that her apparently casual mention of Mr Campion to the Inspector had been a ruse to get hold of him shocked the innocent policeman. He retaliated by insisting that he must see the witnesses at once. Lady Larradine silenced him with a friendly roar. 'My dear man, you can't.

They've gone for a walk. I always turn men out of the house after Christmas luncheon. They'll soon be back. The Brigadier won't miss his Tree! Ah. Here's Fiona. This is Janice Poole-Poole's daughter, Albert. Isn't she a pretty girl?'

Mr Campion saw Miss Poole-Poole with relief, knowing of old that Oates was susceptible to the type. The newcomer was young and lovely, and even her back-combed hair-do and the fact that she appeared to have painted herself two black eyes failed to spoil the exquisite smile she bestowed on the helpless officer.

'Fabulous to have you really here,' she said and sounded as if she really meant it. While he was still recovering, Lady Larradine led him to the window.

'You can't see it because it's pitch dark,' she said, 'but out there, down the garden, there's a wall and it was over it that the Brigadier and Mr Taunton spoke to Mr Sampson at six o'clock last night. No one liked the man Sampson. I think poor Mr Taunton was almost afraid of him. Certainly he seems to have died very untidily!'

'But he did buy Mr Taunton's Christmas gifts for him?'

The dragon lifted a webby eyelid. 'You have already been told that. At six last night Mr Taunton and the Brigadier went to meet him to get the box. I got them into their mufflers so I know! I had the packing paper ready too, for Mr Taunton to take up to his room ... Rather a small one on the third floor.' She lowered her voice to reduce it to the volume of distant traffic. 'Not many pennies but a dear little man!'

'Did you see these presents, Ma'am?'

'Not before they were wrapped! That would have spoiled the surprise!'

'I shall have to see them.' There was a mulish note in the Superintendent's voice which the lady was too experienced to ignore. 'I've thought how to do that without upsetting anybody,' she said brightly. 'The Brigadier and I will cut the presents from the Tree and Fiona will be handing them round. All Mr Taunton's little gifts are in the very distinctive black and gold paper I bought from Millie's Boutique and so, Fiona, you must give every package in gold and black paper not to the person to whom it is addressed but to the Superintendent. Can you do that, dear?'

Miss Poole-Poole seemed to feel the task difficult but not impossible, and the trusting smile she gave Oates cut short his objections like the sun melting frost.

'Splendid!' The Dragon's roar was hearty. 'Give me your arm, Superintendent. You shall take me down.'

As the procession reached the hall it ran into the Brigadier himself. He was a large, pink man, affable enough, but of a martial type and he bristled at the Superintendent. 'Extraordinary time to do your business – middle of Christmas Day!' he said after acknowledging the introductions.

Oates inquired if he had enjoyed his walk.

'Talk?' said the Brigadier. 'I've not been talking. I've been asleep in the card-room. Where's old Taunton?'

'He went for a walk, Athole dear,' bellowed the Dragon gaily.

'So he did. You sent him! Poor feller.'

As the old soldier led the way to the open door of the drawing-room it occurred to both the visitors that the secret of Lady Larradine's undoubted attraction for him lay in the fact that he could hear *her* if no one else. The discovery cast a new light altogether on the story of the encounter with Sampson in the garden.

Meanwhile they had entered the drawing-room and the party had begun. As Mr Campion glanced at the company, ranged in a full circle round a magnificent tree loaded with gifts and sparkling like a waterfall, he saw face after familiar face. They were old acquaintances of the dizzy nineteen-thirties whom he had mourned as gone forever when he thought of them at all. Yet here they all were, not only alive but released by great age from many of the restraints of convention. He noticed that every type of head-gear from night-cap to tiara was being sported with fine individualistic enthusiasm. But Lady Larradine gave him no time to look about. She proceeded with her task immediately.

Each guest had been provided with a small invalid table beside his armchair, and Oates, reluctant but wax in Fiona's hands, was no exception. He found himself seated between a mountain in flannel and a wraith in mauve mink, waiting his turn with the same beady-eyed avidity.

Christmas tree procedure at the Ccraven proved to be well organised. The Dragon did little work herself. Armed with a swagger stick, she merely prodded parcel after parcel hanging amid the boughs, while the task of detaching them was performed by the Brigadier, who handed them to Fiona. Either to add to the excitement or perhaps to muffle any unfortunate comment on gifts received by the uninhibited company, jolly Christmas music was played throughout, and under cover of the noise Mr Campion was able to tackle his hostess.

'Where is Taunton?' he whispered.

'Such a nice little man. Most presentable but just a little teenyweeny bit dishonest.' Lady Larradine ignored his question but continued to put him in the picture at speed, whilst supervising the Tree at the same time. 'Fifty-seven convictions, I believe, but only small ones. I only got it all out of him last week. Shattering! He'd been so *useful* amusing the Brigadier. When he came he looked like a lost soul with no luggage, but after no time at all he settled in perfectly.' She paused and stabbed at a ball of coloured cellophane with her stick before returning to her startled guest.

'Albert, I am terribly afraid poor Mr Taunton took that dreadful jewellery of Maisie Phaeton's. It appears to have been entirely her fault. He was merely wandering past her house, feeling in need of care and attention. The door was wide open and he found himself inside, picking up a few odds and ends. When he discovered from all that fuss in the newspapers what it was he had got hold of – how well known it was, I mean – he was quite horrified and had to hide. And where better than here with us where he never had to go out?'

'Where indeed!' Mr Campion dared not glance across the room to where the Superintendent was unwrapping his black and gold parcels. 'Where is he now?'

'Of course, I hadn't the faintest idea what was worrying the man until he confessed,' the Dragon went on stonily. 'Then I realised that something would have to be done at once to protect everybody. The wretch had hidden all that frightful stuff in our tool shed for three months, not daring to keep it in the house, and to make matters worse, the impossible person at the end of the garden, Mr Sampson, had recognised him and *would* keep speaking. Apparently people in the – er – underworld all know each other just as those of us in – er – other closed circles do.'

Mr Campion, whose hair was standing on end, had a moment of inspiration. 'This absurd rigmarole about Taunton getting Sampson to buy him some Christmas gifts wholesale was your idea!' he said accusingly.

The Dragon stared. 'It seemed the best way of getting Maisie's jewellery back to her without any one person being solely involved,' she said frankly. 'I knew we should all recognise the things the moment we saw them, and I was certain that after a lot of argument we should decide to pack them up and send them round to her. But, if there *was* any repercussion, we should *all* be in it (quite a formidable array, dear) and the blame could be traced to Mr Sampson if absolutely necessary. You see, the Brigadier is convinced that Sampson *was* there last night. Mr Taunton very cleverly left him on the lawn and went behind the tool shed and came back with the box.'

'How completely immoral!'

The Dragon had the grace to look embarrassed. 'I don't think the Sampson angle would ever have arisen,' she said. 'But if it had, Sampson was quite a terrible person. Almost a blackmailer. Utterly dishonest and inconsiderate. Think how he has spoiled everything and endangered us all by getting himself killed on the one afternoon when we said he was here, so that the police were brought in. Just the one thing I was trying to avoid. When the Inspector appeared this morning I was so upset I thought of you!'

In his not unnatural alarm Mr Campion so far forgot himself as to touch her sleeve. 'Where is Taunton now?'

The Dragon threshed her train. 'Really, boy! What a fidget you are! If you must know, I gave him his Christmas present – every penny I had in cash for he was broke again, he told me – and sent him for a nice long walk after lunch. Having seen the Inspector here this morning he was glad to go.' She paused and a gentle gleam came into her hooded eyes. 'If that Superintendent has the stupidity to try to find him when Maisie has her monstrosities back none of us will be able to identify him I'm afraid. And there's another thing. If the Brigadier should be forced to give evidence I am sure he will stick to his guns about Mr Sampson being down the garden here at six o'clock last night. He believes he was. That would mean that someone very wicked would have to go unpunished, wouldn't it? Sampson was a terrible person but no one should have killed him.'

Mr Campion was silenced. He glanced fearfully across the room.

The Superintendent was seated at his table wearing the strained yet slap-happy expression of a man with concussion. On his left was a pile of black and gilt wrappings, on his right a rajah's ransom in somewhat specialised form. From where he stood Mr Campion could see two examples amid the rest: a breastplate in gold, pearl and enamel in the shape of a unicorn in a garden and an item which looked like a plover's egg in tourmaline encased in a ducal coronet. There was also a soapstone monkey and a silver paper-knife.

Much later that evening Mr Campion and the Superintendent drove quietly back to headquarters. Oates had a large cardboard box on his knee. He clasped it tenderly.

He had been silent for a long time when a thought occurred to him.

'Why did they take him into the house in the first place?' he said. 'An elderly crook looking lost! No luggage!'

Mr Campion's pale eyes flickered behind his spectacles.

'Don't forget the Duchess's housekeeping money,' he murmured. 'I should think he offered one of the widows who really run that place the first three months' payment in cash, wouldn't you? That must be an impressive phenomenon in that sort of business, I fancy.'

Oates caught his breath and fell silent once more until presently he burst out again.

'Those people! That woman!' he exploded. 'When they were younger they led me a pretty dance – losing things or getting themselves swindled. But now they're old they take the blessed biscuit! Do you see how she's tied my hands, Campion?'

Mr Campion tried not to grin.

'Snapdragons are just permissible at Christmas,' he said. 'Handled with extreme caution, they burn very few fingers it seems to me.' He tapped the cardboard box. 'And some of them provide a few plums for retiring coppers, don't they, Superintendent?'

Let Nothing You Dismay!

Ellis Peters

The girl in the patched jeans and the voluminous black sweater got off the bus from Comerbourne at the stop opposite the Sitting Duck at ten minutes past seven in the evening, on the twenty-third of December. It was too early then for the landlord to be doing much business in the bar, too late for any delayed shoppers or honest folk coming home from work to be about the single street of the village, and only one other passenger descended from the ancient bus, and scurried away at once into the darkness, to vanish with the crisp click of a gate-latch and in through a house door just beyond the pub. There was no one to notice the arrival of the girl in Mottisham, and by the time the bus rattled away up the valley road towards its final halt at Abbot's Bale, a mile further towards the Welsh border, she, too, had vanished into the tree-shrouded darkness of the lane that climbed the slope behind the church.

The long cleft of Middlehope climbs the valley of a border stream, dwindling as it mounts, until the river shrinks into the spring that is its source, the final village of Abbot's Bale is left behind and nothing remains but the bare moorland and occasional marsh of the watershed between England and Wales. The local bus, family-owned and -driven, turns about at Abbot's Bale after its final evening run, the driver has a meal, a break, a gossip and a single pint at the Gun Dog before driving back down the valley to Comerbourne, which is home. Why go further? Over the two bleak miles of the crest there are no houses to be served. The road goes on, and winds its way down to civilisation again on the other side, but for practical purposes Abbot's Bale is the end of the road.

Even at the more congenial level of the village of Mottisham, population is still sparse, in spite of some new development on the lower slopes, and there was no one abroad to see or hear the girl in the patched jeans as she walked briskly up the winding lane, past one or two lighted cottage windows, towards one of the older houses on the fringe of the village. She was small and lightly built, almost silent on the unpaved road surface, almost invisible in her dark clothing. The night was moonless and overcast, relatively mild for December, though there might well be frost later, in the small hours.

She had left the few lights of the village behind, and the stone wall of a well-treed garden began on her right hand. Fifty yards along the wall was pierced by a modest, square-pillared gateway, its white gate wide open on a drive flanked by old shrubberies. The girl turned in there, and proceeded confidently up the drive until it curved to the left, and for the first time brought into view, clear-cut against the sky and rearing out of the cloudy shapelessness of old trees, the line of the roof and the square bulk of the upper part of the house. A solid, respectable, middle-class house, probably mid-Victorian, a silhouette cut out in black paper against a mount just perceptibly less black. And profoundly silent, to the point of menace.

The girl halted in the cover of the trees, and stood a moment perfectly still, contemplating the unrelieved darkness. Not a light in the entire bulk, outside or in. Even the heaviest of curtains could hardly have sealed in light totally, had there been any to conceal. Still, you never know! The girl marched on boldly, climbed the steps to the front door, and rang the bell. For a moment she stood listening, an ear inclined to the door, but not a sound of any kind responded from within. Appearances were confirmed; the house was empty.

She descended the steps again, and without hesitation set off by the path that rounded the corner of the house, and made for the back premises. Evidently she already knew the ground well enough to know where she could find what she wanted. The garden was old, closely treed, cover available close to the walls on every side but the front. Round at the rear there was a small, rather high window, the kind to be found in cloakroom or scullery or larder, and this one probably as old as the house, never replaced by a more modern and more secure one. Under the bushes that crowded near it the girl dumped the duffle bag from her shoulder, rummaged inside its outer pocket for a moment and produced a long nail-file. Reaching the latch of the window was no problem. An old creeper that covered half of the rear wall had its formidable roots braced almost under the sill, and took her light weight without a quiver as she climbed nimbly to the casement and levered the file in beneath the latch. It rose obligingly easily, and she drew the window open, held by the gnarled stem of the creeper, and slid one slim leg over the sill. The rest of her small person folded itself neatly and followed, and a moment later she was standing on the tiled floor of a small room, apparently a cloakroom, listening to the silence as it settled again gradually after the small agitation of her own movements.

She was in, and she had the house to herself.

Moving with unruffled confidence, she let herself out into a dark passage, and felt her way along it with fingertips brushing the walls, past a kitchen door and towards the front of the house. By this time her eyes were becoming sufficiently accustomed to the darkness to distinguish faintly the broad sweep of the banister rail of the staircase in the wide Victorian hall, and feeling her way along the wall parallel to it she found the light-switch, and was hesitating with her finger on it when the first slight, disturbing sound came to her ears, and she froze where she stood, listening intently.

A car's engine, quiet and distant as yet, but not so distant as to be on the main road, on the other side of the house from the narrow lane by which she had come. It was coming gradually nearer, cutting through from that road by the short piece that would bring it round to the lane, and to the gate. Her acute ear caught the check and change in the note as it turned into the drive, and the sudden cautious crescendo as it rounded the curve. No doubt about it, someone was at this moment driving up to the front door – No, correction! – *past* the front door, and on round to the right, deep into the cover of the trees. Wheeling, backing and turning now. Ready for a quick departure?

The girl took her finger hastily from the light-switch instead of pressing it, swooped round the ornate newel-post and went scrambling up the stairs, hands spread to feel her way, and into the first bedroom on that side of the house. The large window showed as a shape of comparative pallor, the curtains undrawn, and prolonged acquaintance with the night had given her a fair measure of vision by this time. Peering down into the open between the house and its encircling trees, she could distinguish movement and form even when the car lights were switched off. Not a car, though, a van, middle-sized, elderly, backed unobtrusively into cover before it halted. And a minute later, after profound, listening silence, the cab doors opened quietly, and two figures slid out and crossed like shifting shadows to the window immediately below the one where she crouched in hiding.

One of them spoke, but it was only a wordless murmur. But when the second figure stepped back briefly to look up at the face of the house she saw that he carried something under his arm, and the something had the unmistakable shape of a gun. Shotguns they were carrying, these days, and this was the precise outline of a man with a shotgun, used to it, and probably all too ready to use it at the drop of a hat. A flicker of light reflected briefly from under the wall. They had a torch, and were using it to locate the fastenings of the window. A minute later she heard the sharp, tinkling fall of glass. They were in the house with her.

She took a moment to consider both the room she was in and the alarming possibilities. They had brought a van: that meant larger plunder, pieces of furniture, antiques, silver. But not a very large van, not the kind to accommodate half the contents of the house. They were after chosen pieces. Probably they knew already what they wanted, collectors' pieces, whatever they had customers for, or could most profitably find customers for. Professionals specialised, handling only what they knew best. And here she was in a bedroom filled with good furniture, and she had better not stay there, if she could find a less likely place to provide desirable loot. And meantime ...

She crossed the room to the dressing-table, detected by the ghostly gleam of mirrors. Where they found the light to reflect as they did she had no time to consider. She found what she was searching for in the second drawer, a roll of soft Indian leather as thick as her wrist, tied with brocaded ribbons. Without staying to untie it and confirm what was within, she could feel the shapes of bracelet and brooch and necklace through the silky folds. With luck they wouldn't even look for this, if clocks and china were what they fancied, but she meant at all costs to retain it if she could. She stuffed it down the neck of her sweater, made for the door and opened it cautiously to listen for what was happening below.

They had not ventured to put on a light, but seemed to know, even by the beam of a torch, carefully shaded, exactly where to find what they wanted. There were voices now, subdued but audible, one gravelly, laconic and professionally calm, one sharp and edgy, and distinctly disquieting in its suggestion of hair-trigger nervousness.

'Take this an' all, eh?' He was close under the stairs, handling glass by the sound of it, but still with the gun under his arm. The gravelly voice swore at him, but still low and placidly.

'No, leave it! Come on with this clock 'ere, and look sharp.'

The edgy one came, as ordered, but still mutinous. 'What you turning it up for? That's good stuff.'

'Good stuff, but no buyer. Stick to what I know. Safer.'

And there went the clock aforesaid, out through the open window, to be stowed away in the van. They were working fast and methodically. The two of them, now, were carrying a piece of furniture between them, very carefully. Some sort of cabinet. They were in and out of other rooms, there was no moment when she had any chance to steal down the stairs in their absence, and get back to the rear of the house, and the open cloakroom window. She would have to sit it out, somewhere as safe as possible, and hope for them to go. How if they decided to come and continue their hunt upstairs?

The girl retreated warily along the dark landing, feeling her way against the wall. Down below her the shaded torch beam focused on the foot of the stairs.

'What's up there?' demanded the nervous voice, uneasy about time passing.

'His coins. Worth a packet sold in one go.'

'Dead risky!' hazarded the doubter, but he was already on the stairs.

'Got it all set up, safe as houses. They're going west.'

The girl felt behind her, softly opened the rearmost bedroom door, let herself in with feverish haste and closed it behind her. Flattened against the wall behind the door, she heard them enter the bedroom she had quitted. There were a few minutes of silence, and then the sound of wood splintering, and a murmur of satisfaction. They had got what they had come for. Collectors sometimes allow their pride and joy to be viewed and recorded, whether in professional journals or regional television news programmes, and expert thieves digest and remember every detail. But now surely they would leave, and she could make her own departure once they were clear of the house.

They were out on the landing again with their loot, they must be nearly as eager to leave as she was to hear them go.

'What else they got up here, then?' wondered the edgy voice, turning towards where she hid, instead of away. 'Might as well take a look.'

'We got what we know we can deal with,' said his mentor sharply. 'Doesn't pay to take risks out of your depth. Come on, let's get out of here.'

A hand grasped the outer knob of the door. The girl gripped its fellow on her side with both hands and all her strength, and struggled to prevent it from turning. It seemed that his touch had been no more than tentative, and for a moment she managed to hold it fast. But that was her undoing, for at once he said, with rising interest: 'Locked! Let's have a go, then!' and she heard him lay his shotgun aside, leaning it against the jamb of the door to have both hands free. The next moment the knob turned, jerking her hands away, his shoulder thudded heavily against the wood, and the door flew open so violently that he shot half across the room, and let out a yell, suddenly thrown off-balance.

The door, flung back hard against the girl's body, rebounded again with a dull sound that should have covered the gasp the blow fetched out of her, but did not quite cover it. The professional of these two had acute hearing. In his business he needed it.

'Hi up! What's here?' He was inside with them in an instant, the shotgun braced under his right arm, the torch in his left, sweeping the room. He kicked the door shut, and spread both feet firmly to bring the barrel of the gun to bear on the intruder. There was one instant when the girl gave herself up for lost, and as instantly recovered when the alarm point passed and nothing happened. All over in about half a second. Thank God it was the professional, not the lout, who held the gun, and his nerves were considerably stouter than his colleague's, and his wits quicker. The beam of the torch swept the girl from head to foot, and the most danger- ous moment was past. Not that she could reckon on that as the end of danger, but at least it hadn't wiped her out on sight.

'Well, well!' said the expert, slowly lowering the barrel of the gun, but holding her pinned in the ray of the torch. 'Look what we've found!'

His mate was certainly looking, dumbstruck and plainly in a state of panic which would have been her death if he had been holding the gun. 'My Gawd!' he babbled, still breath- less and splayed against the wall. 'How come she's here? You said they was gone for hours. What we goin' to do with 'er now? She 'as to go, or we're goners. What you waitin' for? We *got* to ... '

'Shut up!' said the elder shortly. And to the girl, standing mute and still and very wary in the beam of the torch: 'Who the hell are you?'

She had a vague view of them both now, at least their bulk and shape, even glimpses of features in the diffused light. The older man was stocky and square and shaggy, in what seemed to be overalls and a donkey jacket, mid-dle-aged and composed, even respectable-looking, like an honest transport driver working late, a good appearance for a professional burglar. The other one was young, large, unshaven and lumpish, with a general bearing between a cringe and a swagger. Hard to account for why so competent a pro should tolerate so perilous and probably unreliable an aide. Perhaps they were father and son, and there wasn't much choice, or perhaps the lout had his own peculiar skills, like breaking open doors, or battering people to death if they got in the way. Anyhow, there they were, and she was stuck with them.

'Well, I'm not the missus, here,' she said, venturing close to sounding tart, 'that's for sure. Nor the parlour maid, neither.'

'No, you for sure ain't,' allowed the interrogator. 'So what are you doing here?'

'Same as you, if I'd had the chance,' she said resignedly. 'If you hadn't come butting in I'd have been off a long time ago. You're one of a kind yourself, it seems, you should know another when you see one. What else you think I'd be doing here?'

'You reckon?' He was not impressed, but he was willing to think about it. 'You got a name?'

'Not one you'd want to know, no more than I want to

know yours. What's the use of names, anyway, wouldn't mean nothing to you. I told you what you asked me.'

'What you wasting time for?' demanded the younger man feverishly, and laid a hand on the stock of the gun, but his companion held on to it and elbowed him off. 'Get rid of her and let's get out of here. What else can we do with her now? She's nothing but trouble, whoever she is.'

'Shut up!' repeated his elder, and kept his eyes unwaveringly upon the girl. 'Two of a kind, are we?' he repeated thoughtfully. 'How'd you get in here, then? Go on, show me!'

'Through a back window, round by the kitchen. Go on, have a look for yourself. I left it open, ready to get out again quick. Bent me nail-file, levering up the latch. Go on, see for yourself if you don't believe me. I left my duffle bag under the bushes, outside there. Go on, send him to have a look! I'm not telling you lies. Why should I? I got nothing against you. I know nothing, I seen nothing, and sure as hell I'm saying nothing.'

The elder man hesitated for a long minute, and then abruptly jerked head and gun in the direction of the stairs. 'Come on down, and go softly on the way, I'll be right behind. I dunno yet. Go on round the back, Stan, and see. How big is this window, then? I never spotted none we could use.'

'I got through it, didn't I? Show you, if you like.' She was feeling her way down stair by stair ahead of him, only too conscious of the shotgun close behind, and devoutly grateful that it was not in the younger man's hands. '*He's* too big to get through, though. Pays to be a little person, on these capers.'

'You done many?' He was sceptical but open-minded.

'None round here before. Never strike twice in the same place. Like lightning!' she said, testing the water a little deeper.

'Come from round here?'

'Not me! I came in from Brum, tonight. Came up here by the bus, and I aim to go back by the bus. He comes back down the valley about half past nine.'

The young man Stan, however suspicious and uneasy, had done as his chief instructed, and made off ahead across the hall, out through the window they had forced and round to the rear of the house. She felt somewhat reassured in his absence, however brief it might be. This one at least was a professional, and elderly, and professionals who have survived to reach middle age have normally done so by avoiding unnecessary complications like murder.

'How long were you in here ahead of us?' he asked suddenly. They had reached the foot of the stairs, and could hear Stan's steps faintly crisping the gravel outside.

'About a couple of minutes. Frightened me to death when I heard you driving in. I thought the folks were coming home too soon.'

'Get what you come for?'

'Bits and pieces,' she said, after a momentary hesitation. Whatever she said would be a gamble.

'Down the neck of your jumper?' And when she was silent: 'What's your preference, then?'

'You got what *you* come for,' she said, reluctant and aggrieved. 'You wouldn't grudge me a ring or two, would you? I don't trespass on your patch, you might as well leave me mine. What you got to lose? We're both bound to keep our mouths shut, we're in the same boat. I never been inside, and don't intend to go, but you could shop me just as easy as I could you.'

Stan was coming back, sliding in through the open window to dump her duffle bag in front of his leader. 'It was there, sure enough, slung under the bushes. The window, an' all. That's how she got in. So what? You can't trust women.'

'Why not?' she said indignantly. 'We *are* in the same boat. I can't grass on you or anybody without putting my own head on the chopping-block. I broke in, as well as you.'

'It takes some thinking about,' said the elder, 'except we don't have time. Sooner we're out of here, the better.'

'Then that's it,' she agreed firmly. 'So let's get going. And you can give me a lift out to the main road, where the bus stops. Wherever you're heading, you've got to go that far to get started.'

'I say make sure,' insisted Stan. 'If her mouth was shut for good we'd know where we were.'

'Yes, up the creek without a paddle,' said his leader with decision. 'What, with a body to get rid of? I'm driving nowhere with that in the van. Leave it here? It wouldn't be silence you'd be making sure of. If you're ambitious to be a lifer, I'm not. Come on, let's get the van away while we're safe. Pick up your bag, kid, and hop in the cab. Might as well drop you off. Sooner you was in Brum than hanging around these parts.'

In the cab of the van she was glad to see that Stan did not mind taking the wheel. That was a relief. He couldn't very well commit murder while he was driving, and she had the elder man in between.

The first few house lights of the village came into view. At the crossroads she would get down and walk away, still in one piece, still with the soft roll of leather and its contents snugly tucked away inside her sweater.

'Where will you be slipping a catch next?' the man beside her asked, as civilly and normally as if they had just picked up a young hitch-hiker out of the kindness of their hearts, and felt it only courteous to take an interest in her prospects.

'A hundred miles away, for preference,' said the girl. 'I'm going to enjoy my Christmas first. Never work at Christmas. This'll do, drop me off here.'

It was under the light, just opposite the Sitting Duck. She dropped her bag out first, and jumped down after it, lifted a hand in ambiguous acknowledgement and stood a moment to watch which way the van turned into the main valley road. Uphill, towards the border and the watershed. That made sense, small chance of being intercepted on that road on most winter nights.

The van, hitherto just a shape in the dark, took on form as it drew away along the road. The rear number plate was muddy, but perfectly legible.

The girl watched it for only a few seconds. Then she crossed the road and went into the Sitting Duck.

The bus which would presently set off on its last trip of the evening, down the valley and back to Comerbourne, was parked at this hour just aside from the minute open space which was the centre of the village of Abbot's Bale, leaving the green free for an assembled crowd surprisingly large for so apparently modest a community. At this hour of the evening most of the shepherds and hands from all the surrounding farms would in any case have been congregated here in the Gun Dog, but on this evening they had brought wives and families with them, for the church choir was carolsinging for charity on the green, and there was warmth, welcome and the harvest of a dozen farm kitchens to be found in the church hall, on sale at nominal prices for the same good cause that was stretching the lungs of all the local choirboys, and filling the night air with a silver mist of frosty breath. The driver of the bus was sitting in a corner settle in the bar over a pie, along with Sergeant Moon, who was the law in Middlehope, rather than merely representing it, and without whom no function could be a complete success. The driver, a conscientious man, was making his single pint last as long as possible. Or if, for once, he had exceeded it, no one was counting. Sergeant Moon was on his second when the landlord called him to the telephone.

He came back in a few moments to haul the driver out with him into the night, and shortly thereafter the driver was seen to climb into his bus and move it several yards lower down the valley road, clear of the full-throated assembly presently delivering 'The Farewell of the Shepherds' to the listening night, and there to stow it face-forward up the considerable slope of the hedge-bank and abandon it, tail looming over the empty road. At the same time Sergeant Moon was seen to emerge from the yard of the Gun Dog with a red and white traffic cone in either hand, and place them judiciously in the fairway, a few yards below the point where the bus's rear loomed out of the hedge. A third such cone, brought out to join the first pair, completed a sufficient barrier on this narrow road.

The next thing that happened was that a word in the ear of the Reverend Stephen and his choirmaster unaccountably shifted the singers to a position in the middle of the road, instead of neatly grouped on the triangle of green, and effectively blocked the way to all traffic. Their horn lantern, reared on a long pole, stood out like a battle standard in the midst.

They were in the middle of 'Good King Wenceslas', with the leading bass cast as the king and the star treble as the page, when the sound of a motor climbing the slope was heard, and Sergeant Moon, hands benevolently clasped behind his back, and legs braced apart, took his stand in the middle of the road, and turned about at the last moment to confront the battered van with a large hand and a benign smile, as it baulked, hooted and stopped. His pace as he approached it and leaned to the window was leisured, and his smile amiable.

'A happy Christmas to you, too, sir, I'm sure! Sorry to hold you up, but you see how it is. This is for the Salvation Army. They'll be finished pretty soon now, I'm sure you won't mind waiting.'

'Well, we need to get on, officer,' said the elderly man in the passenger seat. 'Got a long way to go yet. You sure they won't be long? You couldn't clear a way through for us?'

The tension within the cab, which had smelled strongly of panic as soon as the window was rolled down, seemed to ease very slightly at the seasonal greeting. The barrier seemed to have nothing to do with anything more menacing than some village choir collecting for charity. Sergeant Moon radiated placid reassurance.

'They can't keep the kids out too late. They'll soon wind it up now. The bus has to leave on time, some of 'em will be travelling down the valley a piece. Soon be on your way now.'

The Sergeant had already located the shotgun, laid along the seat behind the driver and his passenger, and covered from sight with a rug, but the shape of the stock showed through. It would not be simple to produce and level it quickly from that position. All the same, the driver was getting distinctly more jumpy with every second, drumming his fingers on the wheel and twitching his shoulders ominously. The older one was tough enough to sit it out, but he was getting worried about his mate's liability to blow up at any moment. The Sergeant was glad to observe the three or four solid villagers emerge from the yard of the inn and amble innocently into position a few yards down the road. If anyone abandoned ship and ran, it would be in that direction, since there must be some fifty or more people deployed in the road ahead.

'God rest you merry, gentlemen,
Let nothing you dismay ...'

sang the choir imperturbably, embattled round their lantern banner.

The bus driver had climbed into his cab, and was watching with vague, detached interest. The man at the wheel of the van stared ahead, and had begun to sweat and blink, and curse wordlessly, his lips contorting. The older man kicked at him sidewise, and precipitated what he was trying to avoid.

It all happened in a second. The young man loosed the wheel, uttered a howling oath, shoved his mate sideways and grabbed for the shotgun. At the same instant Sergeant Moon waved a hand, and the service bus, brakes released, rolled ponderously but rapidly down the slope of grass, and careered backwards directly towards the front of the van.

A shriller yell followed the first, cutting through the carol with a note of utter hysteria. The shotgun, hurled aside as suddenly as it had been seized, and still somewhat tangled in the rug, went off with a tremendous bang, fortunately spattering nothing more vulnerable than the roof of the van, as Stan fought his gears and tried to back off in a hurry, and failing, stalled his engine, flung open his door and hurtled out and down the road, to be engulfed in the arms of a six-foot shepherd from one of the hill farms, ably supported by the cellarman from the Gun Dog.

'God rest you merry' was never finished. The choir broke ranks with a view halloo, and piled into the affray with enthusiasm, in case the van should yet serve to extricate its remaining occupant, by some feat of trick driving. But the professional knew when he was beaten, and had sense enough not to aggravate matters when they were past mending. The bus had braked to a halt at least a foot short of his right front wing, but still he sat motionless in his place, staring bitterly before him into the unexpected revelry, and cursing with monotonous, resigned fluency under his breath.

Sergeant Moon reached in unresisted, and appropriated the shotgun. Large, interested locals leaned on either door, grinning. The Sergeant moved round to the back of the van, and opened the rear doors.

'Well, well!' he said, gratified. 'Aladdin's cave! Won't the Harrisons be pleased when Father Christmas comes!'

The girl in black silk evening trousers and bat-winged, sequinned top sat, cross-legged, in front of the fire she had kindled in the living room before her uncle and aunt had returned from their dinner party, and recounted the events of the evening for them with relish as she roasted chestnuts. It was no bad start to a Christmas vacation to be able to take her elders' breath away, first with shock and dismay, then with relief and admiration.

'So you see, it's all right, you'll get everything back safely. I did rescue your jewellery, I was determined they shouldn't have that, but all the rest will be back soon. Sergeant Moon has been on the phone already. I knew he'd manage everything, somehow, and I did warn him they had a gun. But isn't it lucky for you that I decided to come down a day early, after all? I did ring you, but you were out already. And anyhow, I knew how I could get in. Now who was it said I'd never make it as an actress?'

'But, for God's sake, girl,' protested her uncle, not yet recovered from multiple shock, 'you might have got yourself killed.'

'Well, that's what I was trying to avoid! I was there, and they found me, I didn't have much choice. When you're cornered, no use coming apart at the seams. You have to use what you've got – same as Sergeant Moon had to do. And I *had* broken in, and I suppose I *did* look every inch the part. Anyhow, they believed it. Finally!' she added, somewhat more sombrely. 'I admit there *were* moments ...'

'But you're taking it all so coolly,' her aunt wondered faintly. 'Weren't you even afraid?'

'Terrified!' said the girl complacently, and fielded a chestnut which had shot out upon the rug. 'But I tell you what – as soon as my folks get back from Canada I'm going to put it to them they should let me switch to drama school. I always said that was my natural home.'

The Lion's Tooth

Edmund Crispin

It lay embedded in crudely wrought silver, with a surround of big lustreless semiprecious stones; graven on the reverse of the silver was an outline which Fen recognised as the ichthys, pass-sign of primitive Christianity.

'Naturally, one thinks of Androcles,' said the reverend mother. 'Or if not of him specially, then of the many other early Christians who faced the lions in the arena.' She paused, then added: 'This, you know, is the convent's only relic. Apparently it is also our only clue.'

She stooped to replace it in the sacristy cupboard; and Fen, while he waited, thought of frail old Sister St Jude, whose only intelligible words since they had found her had been 'The tooth of a lion!', and again – urgently, repeatedly – 'The tooth of a lion!'

He thought, too, of the eleven-year-old girl who had been kidnapped and of her father, who had obstinately refused to divulge to the police the medium through which the ransom was to be paid, for fear that in trying to catch the kidnapper they would blunder and bring about the death of his only child. He would rather pay, he had said; and from this decision he was in no way to be moved ...

It had been the reverend mother who had insisted on consulting Fen; but following her now, as she led the way back to her office, he doubted if there was much he could do. The available facts were altogether too arid and too few. Thus: Francis Merrill was middle-aged, a widower and a wealthy businessman. Two weeks ago, immediately after Christmas, he had gone off to the Continent, leaving his daughter Mary, at her own special request, to the care of the sisters. During the mornings Mary had helped the sisters with their chores. But in the afternoons, with the reverend mother's encouragement, she would usually go out and ramble round the countryside.

On most of these outings Mary Merrill was accompanied, for a short distance, by Sister St Jude. Sister St Jude was ailing; the doctors, however, had decreed that she must get plenty of fresh air, so even through the recent long weeks of frost and ice she had continued to issue forth, well wrapped up, and spend an hour or two each afternoon on a sheltered seat near the summit of the small hill at the convent's back. It had been Mary Merrill's habit to see her settled there and then to wander off on her own.

Until, this last Tuesday, a search-party of the sisters had come upon Sister St Jude sprawled near her accustomed seat with concussion of the brain.

Mary Merrill had not come home that night. The reverend

mother had, of course, immediately notified the police; and Francis Merrill, hastening back from Italy, had found a ransom note awaiting him.

To all intents and purposes, that was all; the police, it seemed, had so far achieved precisely nothing. If only – Fen reflected – if *only* one knew more about the *girl herself:* for instance, where she was likely to have gone, and what she was likely to have done, on these rambles of hers. But Francis Merrill had refused even to meet Fen; and the reverend mother had been unable to produce any information about Mary more specific and instructive than the statement that she had been a friendly, trusting, *ordinary* sort of child …

'I suppose,' said Fen, collapsing into a chair, 'that it's quite certain Sister St Jude has never said anything comprehensible *other* than this phrase about the lion's tooth?'

'Absolutely certain, I am afraid,' the reverend mother replied. 'Apart from a few – a few sounds which may conceivably have been French words, she has not yet been able –'

'*French* words?'

'Yes. I should have mentioned, perhaps, that Sister St Jude is a Frenchwoman.'

'I see,' said Fen slowly. 'I see… Tell me, did she – does she, I mean – speak English at all fluently?'

'Not very fluently, no. She has only been over here a matter of nine months or so. Her vocabulary, for instance, is still rather limited …' The reverend mother hesitated. 'Perhaps you are thinking that the phrase about the lion's tooth may have been, misheard. But she has used it many times, in the presence of many of us – including Sister Bartholomew, who is another Frenchwoman – and we have none of us ever had the least doubt about what the words were.'

'Not misheard,' said Fen pensively. 'But misinterpreted, perhaps ...' Looking up, the reverend mother saw that he was on his feet again. 'Reverend Mother, I have an idea,' he went on. 'Or an inkling, rather. At present I don't at all see how it *applies*. But nonetheless, I think that if you'll excuse me, I'll go now and take a look at the place where Sister St Jude was attacked. There's a certain object to be looked for there, which the police may well have found, but decided to ignore.'

'What kind of object?' the reverend mother asked.

And Fen smiled at her. 'Yellow,' he said. 'Something yellow.'

No prolonged search was needed; there the thing lay, in full view of everyone, as plain as the nose on a policeman's face. In a mood of complacency which the reverend mother could hardly have approved, Fen pocketed it, climbed the remaining distance to the top of the little hill and looked around him. The complacency waned somewhat; from this vantage-point he could see buildings galore. Still, with any luck at all ...

The gods were with him that day; within three hours – three hours of peering over hedges, and of surreptitious trespassing in other people's gardens – he located the particular house he sought. A glance at the local directory, a rapid but rewarding contact with the child population of a neighbouring village and by six o'clock he was ready for action.

The man who answered the knock on the front door was grey-haired, weedy, nervous-seeming; while not unprepossessing, he yet had something of a hungry look. 'Mr Jones?'

said Fen, pushing him back into his own hall before he had time to realise what was happening, and without waiting for a reply, added: 'I've come for the child.'

'The child?' Mr Jones looked blank. 'There's no child here. I'm afraid you've got the wrong house.'

'Indeed I haven't,' said Fen confidently. And even as he spoke, the thin, high scream of a young girl welled up from somewhere on the premises, followed by incoherent, sobbing appeals for help. Fen noted the particular door to which pallid Mr Jones's eyes immediately turned: an interesting door, in that it lay well away from the direction whence the scream had come ...

'Yes, we'll go through there, I think,' said Fen pleasantly; and now there was an automatic pistol in his hand. 'It leads to the cellar, I expect. And since I'm not at all fond of men who try to smash in the skulls of helpless old nuns, you may rely on my shooting you without the slightest hesitation or compunction if you make a single false move.'

Later, when Mr Jones had been taken away by the police, and Mary Merrill, hysterical but otherwise not much harmed, restored to her father, Fen went round to the back garden, where he found an engaging female urchin wandering about eating a large bar of chocolate cream.

'That was jolly good,' he told her, handing over the promised ten-shilling note. 'When you grow up, you ought to go on the stage.'

She grinned at him. 'Some scream, mister, eh?' she said.

'Some scream,' Fen agreed.

And: 'It's obvious,' he said to the reverend mother over

lunch next day, 'that Mary Merrill made friends with Jones soon after she came here, and got into the way of visiting him pretty well every afternoon. No harm in that. But then he found out who her father was and began envisaging the possibility of making some easy money.

'What actually *happened*, I understand, is that Mary, on that last visit, took fright at something odd and constrained in his attitude to her, and succeeded in slipping away while his back was turned. Whereupon he very stupidly followed her (in his car, except for the last bit) and tried to grab her when she was already quite close to home.

'She eluded him again, and ran to Sister St Jude for protection. But by that time Jones had gone too far for retreat to be practicable or safe; so he ran after her, struck Sister St Jude down with his stick and this time really did succeed in capturing Mary, knocking her out and so getting her back to his house.

'Whether the dandelion part of it belongs to that particular afternoon, or to some previous one, one doesn't know, but whichever it was, Sister St Jude clearly *noticed* the flower and equally clearly realised, even in her illness and delirium, that it provided a clue to –'

'Wait, please,' the reverend mother implored him faintly. 'Did I hear you say "dandelion"?'

And Fen nodded. 'Yes, dandelion. English corruption of the French *dent-de-lion* – which of course means a lion's tooth. But Sister St Jude's vocabulary was limited: *she* didn't know the English name for it. Therefore, she translated it literally, forgetting altogether the existence of that confusing, but irrelevant, relic of yours –

'Well, I ask you: a dandelion, in January, after weeks of hard frost! But Mary Merrill had managed to find one; had picked it and then perhaps pushed it into a buttonhole of her frock. As every gardener knows, dandelions are prolific and hardy brutes; but in view of the recent weather, this particular dandelion could really *only* have come from a weed in a hot-house within an hour's walk from here. As soon as I saw Jones's, I was certain it was the right one.'

The reverend mother looked at him. 'You were, were you?' she said.

'Well, no, actually I wasn't certain at all,' Fen admitted. 'But I thought that the luck I'd had up to then would probably hold, and I was tired of tramping about, and anyway I haven't the slightest objection to terrorising innocent householders so long as it's in a good cause ... may I smoke?'

Rumpole and the Spirit of Christmas

John Mortimer

I realised that Christmas was upon us when I saw a sprig of holly over the list of prisoners hung on the wall of the cells under the Old Bailey.

I pulled out a new box of small cigars and found its opening obstructed by a tinselled band on which a scarlet-faced Santa was seen hurrying a sleigh full of carcinoma-packed goodies to the Rejoicing World. I lit one as the lethargic screw, with a complexion the colour of faded Bronco, regretfully left his doorstep sandwich and mug of sweet tea to unlock the gate.

'Good morning, Mr Rumpole. Come to visit a customer?'

'Happy Christmas, officer,' I said as cheerfully as possible. 'Is Mr Timson at home?'

'Well, I don't believe he's slipped down to his little place in the country.'

Such were the pleasantries that were exchanged between us legal hacks and discontented screws: jokes that no doubt have changed little since the turnkeys locked the door at Newgate to let in a pessimistic advocate, or the cells under the Colosseum were opened to admit the unwelcome news of the Imperial thumbs-down.

'My Mum wants me home for Christmas.'

'Which Christmas?' It would have been an unreasonable remark and I refrained from it. Instead, I said, 'All things are possible.'

As I sat in the interviewing room, an Old Bailey Hack of some considerable experience, looking through my brief and inadvertently using my waistcoat as an ashtray, I hoped I wasn't on another loser. I had had a run of bad luck during that autumn season, and young Edward Timson was part of that huge South London family whose criminal activities provided such welcome grist to the Rumpole mill. The charge in the seventeen-year-old Eddie's case was nothing less than wilful murder.

'We're in with a chance though, Mr Rumpole, ain't we?'

Like all his family, young Timson was a confirmed optimist. And yet, of course, the merest outsider in the Grand National, the hundred-to-one shot, is in with a chance, and nothing is more like going round the course at Aintree than living through a murder trial. In this particular case, a fanatical prosecutor named Wrigglesworth, known to me as the Mad Monk, was to represent Beechers and Mr Justice Vosper, a bright but wintry-hearted Judge who always felt it his duty to lead for the prosecution, was to play the part of a particularly menacing fence at the Canal Turn.

'A chance. Well, yes, of course you've got a chance, if they can't establish common purpose, and no one knows which of you bright lads had the weapon.'

No doubt the time had come for a brief glance at the prosecution case, not an entirely cheering prospect. Eddie, also known as 'Turpin' Timson, lived in a kind of decaying barracks, a sort of high-rise Lubianka, known as Keir Hardie Court, somewhere in South London, together with his parents, his various brothers and his thirteen-year-old sister, Noreen. This particular branch of the Timson family lived on the thirteenth floor. Below them, on the twelfth, lived the large clan of the O'Dowds. The war between the Timsons and the O'Dowds began, it seems, with the casting of the Nativity play at the local comprehensive school.

Christmas comes earlier each year, and the school show was planned about September. When Bridget O'Dowd was chosen to play the lead in the face of strong competition from Noreen Timson, an incident occurred comparable in historical importance to the assassination of an obscure Austrian archduke at Sarajevo. Noreen Timson announced, in the playground, that Bridget O'Dowd was a spotty little tart quite unsuited to play any role of which the most notable characteristic was virginity.

Hearing this, Bridget O'Dowd kicked Noreen Timson behind the anthracite bunkers. Within a few days war was declared between the Timson and O'Dowd children, and a present of lit fireworks was posted through the O'Dowd front door. On what is known as the 'night in question', reinforcements of O'Dowds and Timsons arrived in old bangers from a number of South London addresses and battle was joined on the stone staircase, a bleak terrain of peeling walls scrawled with graffiti, blowing empty Coca-Cola tins and torn newspapers. The weapons seemed to have been articles in general domestic use such as bread knives, carving knives, broom handles and a heavy screwdriver.

At the end of the day it appeared that the upstairs flat had repelled the invaders, and Kevin O'Dowd lay on the stairs. Having been stabbed with a slender and pointed blade, he was in a condition to become known as the 'deceased' in the case of the Queen against Edward Timson. I made an application for bail for my client, which was refused, but a speedy trial was ordered.

So even as Bridget O'Dowd was giving her Virgin Mary at the comprehensive, the rest of the family was waiting to give evidence against Eddie Timson in that home of British drama, Number 1 Court at the Old Bailey.

'I never had no cutter, Mr Rumpole. Straight up, I never had one,' the defendant told me in the cells. He was an appealing-looking lad with soft brown eyes, who had already won the heart of the highly susceptible lady who wrote his social inquiry report. ('Although the charge is a serious one, this is a young man who might respond well to a period of probation.' I could imagine the steely contempt in Mr Justice Vosper's eye when he read that.)

'Well, tell me, Edward. Who had?'

'I never seen no cutters on no one, honest I didn't. We wasn't none of us tooled up, Mr Rumpole.'

'Come on, Eddie. Someone must have been. They say even young Noreen was brandishing a potato peeler.'

'Not me, honest.'

'What about your sword?'

There was one part of the prosecution evidence that I found particularly distasteful. It was agreed that on the previous Sunday morning, Eddie 'Turpin' Timson had appeared on the stairs of Keir Hardie Court and flourished what appeared to be an antique cavalry sabre at the assembled O'Dowds, who were just popping out to Mass.

'Me sword I bought up the Portobello? I didn't have that there, honest.'

'The prosecution can't introduce evidence about the sword. It was an entirely different occasion.' Mr Bernard, my instructing solicitor, who fancied himself as an infallible lawyer, spoke with a confidence which I couldn't feel. He, after all, wouldn't have to stand up on his hind legs and argue the legal toss with Mr Justice Vosper.

'It rather depends on who's prosecuting us. I mean, if it's some fairly reasonable fellow ...'

'I think,' Mr Bernard reminded me, shattering my faint optimism and ensuring that we were all in for a very rough Christmas indeed, 'I think it's Mr Wrigglesworth. Will he try to introduce the sword?'

I looked at 'Turpin' Timson with a kind of pity. 'If it is the Mad Monk, he undoubtedly will.'

When I went into Court, Basil Wrigglesworth was standing with his shoulders hunched up round his large, red ears, his gown dropped to his elbows, his bony wrists protruding from the sleeves of his frayed jacket, his wig pushed back and his huge hands joined on his lectern in what seemed to be an attitude of devoted prayer. A lump of cottonwool clung to his chin where he had cut himself shaving. Although well into his sixties, he preserved a look of boyish clumsiness. He appeared, as he always did when about to prosecute on a charge carrying a major punishment, radiantly happy.

'Ah, Rumpole,' he said, lilting his eyes from the police verbals as though they were his breviary. 'Are you defending *as usual*?'

'Yes, Wrigglesworth. And you're prosecuting *as usual*?' It wasn't much of a riposte, but it was all I could think of at the time.

'Of course, I don't defend. One doesn't like to call witnesses who may not be telling the truth.'

'You must have a few unhappy moments then, calling certain members of the Constabulary.'

'I can honestly tell you, Rumpole,' his curiously innocent blue eyes looked at me with a sort of pain, as though I had questioned the doctrine of the immaculate conception, 'I have never called a dishonest policeman.'

'Yours must be a singularly simple faith, Wrigglesworth.'

'As for the Detective Inspector in this case,' Counsel for the prosecution went on, 'I've known Wainwright for years. In fact, this is his last trial before he retires. He could no more invent a verbal against a defendant than fly.'

Any more on that tack, I thought, and we should soon be debating how many angels could dance on the point of a pin.

'Look here, Wrigglesworth. That evidence about my

client having a sword: it's quite irrelevant. I'm sure you'd
agree.'

'Why is it irrelevant?' Wrigglesworth frowned.

'Because the murder clearly wasn't done with an antique
cavalry sabre. It was done with a small, thin blade.'

'If he's a man who carries weapons, why isn't that
relevant?'

'A man? Why do you call him a man? He's a child. A boy
of seventeen!'

'Man enough to commit a serious crime.'

'*If* he did.'

'If he didn't, he'd hardly be in the dock.'

'That's the difference between us, Wrigglesworth,' I told
him. 'I believe in the presumption of innocence. You believe
in original sin. Look here, old darling.' I tried to give the
Mad Monk a smile of friendship and became conscious of
the fact that it looked, no doubt, like an ingratiating sneer.
'Give us a chance. You won't introduce the evidence of the
sword, will you?'

'Why ever not?'

'Well,' I told him, 'the Timsons are an industrious family
of criminals. They work hard, they never go on strike. If it
weren't for people like the Timsons, you and I would be out
of a job.'

'They sound in great need of prosecution and punishment. Why shouldn't I tell the jury about your client's
sword? Can you give me one good reason?'

'Yes,' I said, as convincingly as possible.

'What is it?' He peered at me, I thought, unfairly.

'Well, after all,' I said, doing my best, 'it is Christmas.'

It would be idle to pretend that the first day in Court went well, although Wrigglesworth restrained himself from mentioning the sword in his opening speech, and told me that he was considering whether or not to call evidence about it the next day. I cross-examined a few members of the clan O'Dowd on the presence of lethal articles in the hands of the attacking force. The evidence about this varied, and weapons came and went in the hands of the inhabitants of number twelve as the witnesses were blown hither and thither in the winds of Rumpole's cross-examination. An interested observer from one of the other flats spoke of having seen a machete.

'Could that terrible weapon have been in the hands of Mr Kevin O'Dowd, the deceased in this case?'

'I don't think so.'

'But can you rule out the possibility?'

'No, I can't rule it out,' the witness admitted, to my temporary delight.

'You can never rule out the possibility of anything in this world, Mr Rumpole. But he doesn't think so. You have your answer.'

Mr Justice Vosper, in a voice like a splintering iceberg, gave me this unwelcome Christmas present. The case wasn't going well but at least, by the end of the first day, the Mad Monk had kept out all mention of the sword. The next day he was to call young Bridget O'Dowd, fresh from her triumph in the Nativity play.

'I say, Rumpole. I'd be *so* grateful for a little help.'

I was in Pommeroy's Wine Bar, drowning the sorrows

of the day in my usual bottle of the cheapest Château Fleet Street (made from grapes which, judging from the bouquet, might have been not so much trodden as kicked to death by sturdy peasants in gumboots) when I looked up to see Wrigglesworth, dressed in an old mackintosh, doing business with Jack Pommeroy at the sales counter. When I crossed to him, he was not buying the jumbo-sized bottle of ginger beer which I imagined might be his celebratory Christmas tipple, but a tempting and respectably aged bottle of Château Pichon-Longueville.

'What can I do for you, Wrigglesworth?'

'Well, as you know, Rumpole, I live in Croydon.'

'Happiness is given to few of us on this earth,' I said piously.

'And the Anglican Sisters of St Agnes, Croydon, are anxious to buy a present for their Bishop,' Wrigglesworth explained. 'A dozen bottles for Christmas. They've asked my advice, Rumpole. I know so little of wine. You wouldn't care to try this for me? I mean, if you're not especially busy.'

'I should be hurrying home to dinner.' My wife, Hilda (She Who Must Be Obeyed), was laying on rissoles and frozen peas, washed down by my last bottle of Pommeroy's extremely ordinary. 'However, as it's Christmas, I don't mind helping you out, Wrigglesworth.'

The Mad Monk was clearly quite unused to wine. As we sampled the claret together, I saw the chance of getting him to commit himself on the vital question of the evidence of the sword, as well as absorbing an unusually decent bottle. After the Pichon-Longueville I was kind enough to help him by sampling a Boyd-Cantenac and then I said, 'Excellent, this. But of course the Bishop might be a Burgundy man. The nuns might care to invest in a decent Mâcon.'

'Shall we try a bottle?' Wrigglesworth suggested. 'I'd be grateful for your advice.'

'I'll do my best to help you, my old darling. And while we're on the subject, that ridiculous bit of evidence about young Timson and the sword ...'

'I remember you saying I shouldn't bring that out because it's Christmas.'

'Exactly.' Jack Pommeroy had uncorked the Mâcon and it was mingling with the claret to produce a feeling of peace and goodwill towards men. Wrigglesworth frowned, as though trying to absorb an obscure point of theology.

'I don't quite see the relevance of Christmas to the question of your man Timson threatening his neighbours with a sword ...'

'Surely, Wrigglesworth,' I knew my prosecutor well, 'you're of a religious disposition?' The Mad Monk was the product of some bleak Northern Catholic boarding school. He lived alone, and no doubt wore a hair shirt under his black waistcoat, and was vowed to celibacy. The fact that he had his nose deep into a glass of Burgundy at the moment was due to the benign influence of Rumpole.

'I'm a Christian, yes.'

'Then practise a little Christian tolerance.'

'Tolerance towards evil?'

'Evil?' I asked. 'What do you mean, evil?'

'Couldn't that be your trouble, Rumpole? That you really don't recognise evil when you see it.'

'I suppose,' I said, 'evil might be locking up a seventeen-year-old during Her Majesty's pleasure, when Her Majesty may very probably forget all about him, banging him up with a couple of hard and violent cases and their own chamber pots for twenty-two hours a day, so he won't come out till he's a real, genuine, middle-aged murderer ...'

'I did hear the Reverend Mother say,' Wrigglesworth was gazing vacantly at the empty Mâcon bottle, 'that the Bishop likes his glass of port.'

'Then in the spirit of Christmas tolerance I'll help you to sample some of Pommeroy's Light and Tawny.'

A little later, Wrigglesworth held up his port glass in a reverent sort of fashion.

'You're suggesting, are you, that I should make some special concession in this case because it's Christmas time?'

'Look here, old darling.' I absorbed half my glass, relishing the gentle fruitiness and the slight tang of wood. 'If you spent your whole life in that high-rise hellhole called Keir Hardie Court, if you had no fat prosecutions to occupy your attention and no prospect of any job at all, if you had no sort of occupation except war with the O'Dowds ...'

'My own flat isn't particularly comfortable. I don't know a great deal about *your* home life, Rumpole, but you don't seem to be in a tearing hurry to experience it.'

'*Touché*, Wrigglesworth, my old darling.' I ordered us a couple of refills of Pommeroy's port to further postpone the encounter with She Who Must Be Obeyed and her rissoles.

'But we don't have to fight to the death on the staircase,' Wrigglesworth pointed out.

'We don't have to fight at all, Wrigglesworth.'

'As your client did.'

'As my client *may* have done. Remember the presumption of innocence.'

'This is rather funny, this is.' The prosecutor pulled back his lips to reveal strong, yellowish teeth and laughed appreciatively. 'You know why your man Timson is called "Turpin"?'

'No.' I drank port uneasily, fearing an unwelcome revelation.

'Because he's always fighting with that sword of his. He's called after Dick Turpin, you see, who's always duelling on the television. Do you watch the television, Rumpole?'

'Hardly at all.'

'I watch a great deal of the television, as I'm alone rather a lot.' Wrigglesworth referred to the box as though it were a sort of penance, like fasting or flagellation. 'Detective Inspector Wainwright told me about your client. Rather amusing, I thought it was. He's retiring this Christmas.'

'My client?'

'No. DI Wainwright. Do you think we should settle on this port for the Bishop? Or would you like to try a glass of something else?'

'Christmas,' I told Wrigglesworth severely as we sampled the Cockburn, 'is not just a material, pagan celebration. It's not just an occasion for absorbing superior vintages, old darling. It must be a time when you try to do good, spiritual good, to our enemies.'

'To your client, you mean?'

'And to me.'

'To you, Rumpole?'

'For God's sake, Wrigglesworth!' I was conscious of the

fact that my appeal was growing desperate. 'I've had six losers in a row down the Old Bailey. Can't I be included in any Christmas spirit that's going around?'

'You mean, at Christmas especially it is more blessed to give than to receive?'

'I mean exactly that.' I was glad that he seemed, at last, to be following my drift.

'And you think I might give this case to someone, like a Christmas present?'

'If you care to put it that way, yes.'

'I do not care to put it in *exactly* that way.' He turned his pale blue eyes on me with what I thought was genuine sympathy. 'But I shall try and do the case of *R.* v. *Timson in* the way most appropriate to the greatest feast of the Christian year. It is a time, I quite agree, for the giving of presents.'

When they finally threw us out of Pommeroy's, and after we had considered the possibility of buying the Bishop brandy in the Cock Tavern, and even beer in the Devereux, I let my instinct, like an aged horse, carry me on to the Underground and home to Gloucester Road, and there discovered the rissoles, like some traces of a vanished civilisation, fossilised in the oven. She Who Must Be Obeyed was already in bed feigning sleep. When I climbed in beside her she opened a hostile eye.

'You're drunk, Rumpole!' she said. 'What on earth have you been doing?'

I've been having a legal discussion,' I told her, 'on the subject of the admissibility of certain evidence. Vital, from my client's point of view. And, just for a change, Hilda, I think I've won.'

'Well, you'd better try and get some sleep.' And she added with a sort of satisfaction, 'I'm sure you'll be feeling quite terrible in the morning.'

As with all the grimmer predictions of She Who Must Be Obeyed, this one turned out to be true. I sat in Court the next day with the wig feeling like a lead weight on the brain, and the stiff collar sawing the neck like a blunt execution. My mouth tasted of matured birdcage and from a long way off I heard Wrigglesworth say to Bridget O'Dowd, who stood looking particularly saintly and virginal in the witness box, 'About a week before this did you see the defendant, Edward Timson, on your staircase flourishing any sort of weapon?'

It is no exaggeration to say that I felt deeply shocked and considerably betrayed. After his promise to me, Wrigglesworth had turned his back on the spirit of the great Christmas festival. He came not to bring peace but a sword.

I clambered with some difficulty to my feet. After my forensic efforts of the evening before, I was scarcely in the mood for a legal argument. Mr Justice Vosper looked up in surprise and greeted me in his usual chilly fashion.

'Yes, Mr Rumpole. Do you object to this evidence?'

Of course I object, I wanted to say. It's inhuman, unnecessary, unmerciful and likely to lead to my losing another case. Also, it's clearly contrary to a solemn and binding contract entered into after a number of glasses of the Bishop's putative port. All I seemed to manage was a strangled 'Yes'.

'I suppose Mr Wrigglesworth would say,' Vosper, J, was, as ever, anxious to supply any argument that might not yet have occurred to the prosecution, 'that it is evidence of "system".'

'System?' I heard my voice faintly and from a long way off. 'It may be, I suppose. But the Court has a discretion to omit evidence which may be irrelevant and purely prejudicial.'

'I feel sure Mr Wrigglesworth has considered the matter most carefully and that he would not lead this evidence unless he considered it entirely relevant.'

I looked at the Mad Monk on the seat beside me. He was smiling at me with a mixture of hearty cheerfulness and supreme pity, as though I were sinking rapidly and he had come to administer supreme unction. I made a few ill-chosen remarks to the Court, but I was in no condition, that morning, to enter into a complicated legal argument on the admissibility of evidence.

It wasn't long before Bridget O'Dowd had told a deeply disapproving jury all about Eddie 'Turpin' Timson's sword. 'A man,' the Judge said later in his summing up about young Edward, 'clearly prepared to attack with cold steel whenever it suited him.'

When the trial was over, I called in for refreshment at my favourite watering hole, and there, to my surprise, was my opponent Wrigglesworth, sharing an expensive-looking bottle with Detective Inspector Wainwright, the Officer-in-Charge of the case. I stood at the bar, absorbing a consoling glass of Pommeroy's ordinary, when the DI came up to the bar for cigarettes. He gave me a friendly and maddeningly sympathetic smile.

'Sorry about that, sir. Still, win a few, lose a few. Isn't that it?'

'In my case lately, it's been win a few, lose a lot!'

'You couldn't have this one, sir. You see, Mr Wriggles-worth had promised it to me.'

'He had *what*?'

'Well, I'm retiring, as you know. And Mr Wrigglesworth promised me faithfully that my last case would be a win. He promised me that, in a manner of speaking, as a Christmas present. Great man is our Mr Wrigglesworth, sir, for the spirit of Christmas.'

I looked across at the Mad Monk and a terrible suspicion entered my head. What was all that about a present for the Bishop? I searched my memory and I could find no trace of our having, in fact, bought wine for any sort of cleric. And was Wrigglesworth as inexperienced as he would have had me believe in the art of selecting claret?

As I watched him pour and sniff a glass from his superior bottle, and hold it critically to the light, a horrible suspicion crossed my mind. Had the whole evening's events been nothing but a deception, a sinister attempt to nobble Rumpole, to present him with such a stupendous hangover that he would stumble in his legal argument? Was it all in aid of DI Wainwright's Christmas present?

I looked at Wrigglesworth, and it would be no exaggeration to say the mind boggled. He was, of course, perfectly right about me. I just didn't recognise evil when I saw it.

The Assassins' Club

Nicholas Blake

'No,' thought Nigel Strangeways, looking round the table, 'no one would ever guess.'

Ever since, quarter of an hour ago, they had assembled in the ante-room for sherry, Nigel had been feeling more and more nervous – a nervousness greater than the prospect of having to make an after-dinner speech seemed to warrant. It was true that, as the guest of honour, something more than the usual post-prandial convivialities would be expected of him. And of course the company present would, from its nature, be especially critical. But still, he had done this sort of thing often enough before; he knew he was pretty good at it. Why the acute state of jitters, then? After it was all over, Nigel was tempted to substitute 'foreboding' for 'jitters', to wonder whether he oughtn't to have proclaimed these very curious feelings, like Cassandra, from the house-top – even at the risk of spoiling what looked like being a real peach of a dinner party. After all, the dinner party did get spoiled, anyway, and soon enough, too. But, taking all things into consideration, it probably wouldn't have made any difference.

It was in an attempt to dispel this cloud of uneasiness that Nigel began to play with himself the old game of identity-guessing. There was a curious uniformity amongst the faces of the majority of the twenty-odd diners. The women – there were only three of them – looked homely, humorous, dowdy-and-be-damned-to-it. The men, Nigel finally decided, resembled in the mass sanitary inspectors or very minor Civil Servants. They were most of them rather undersized, and ran to drooping moustaches, gold-rimmed spectacles and a general air of mild ineffectualness. There were exceptions, of course. That elderly man in the middle of the table, with the face of a dyspeptic and superannuated bloodhound – it was not difficult to place him; even without the top hat or the wig with which the public normally associated him, Lord Justice Pottinger could easily be recognised – the most celebrated criminal judge of his generation. Then that leonine, mobile face on his left; it had been as much photographed as any society beauty's; and well it might, for Sir Eldred Travers's golden tongue had – it was whispered – saved as many murderers as Justice Pottinger had hanged. There were one or two other exceptions, such as the dark-haired, poetic-looking young man sitting on Nigel's right and rolling bread-pellets.

'No,' said Nigel, aloud this time, 'no one would possibly guess.'

'Guess what?' inquired the young man.

'The bloodthirsty character of this assembly.' He took up the menu-card, at the top of which was printed in red letters

THE ASSASSINS
Dinner, December 20th

'No,' laughed the young man, 'we don't look like murderers, I must admit – not even murderers by proxy.'

'Good lord! are you in the trade, too?'

'Yes. Ought to have introduced myself. Name of Herbert Dale.'

Nigel looked at the young man with increased interest. Dale had published only two crime novels, but he was already accepted as one of the élite of detective writers; he could not otherwise have been a member of that most exclusive of clubs, the Assassins; for, apart from a representative of the Bench, the Bar and Scotland Yard, this club was composed solely of the princes of detective fiction.

It was at this point that Nigel observed two things – that the hand which incessantly rolled bread-pellets was shaking, and that, on the glossy surface of the menu-card Dale had just laid down, there was a moist finger-mark.

'Are you making a speech, too?' Nigel said.

'Me? Good lord, no. Why?'

'I thought you looked nervous,' said Nigel, in his direct way.

The young man laughed, a little too loudly. And, as though that was some kind of signal, one of those unrehearsed total silences fell upon the company. Even in the street outside, the noises seemed to be damped, as though an enormous soft pedal had been pressed down on everything. Nigel realised that it must have been snowing since he came in. A disagreeable sensation of eeriness crept over him. Annoyed with this sensation – a detective has no right to feel psychic, he reflected angrily, not even a private detective as celebrated as Nigel Strangeways – he forced himself to look round the brilliantly lighted room, the animated yet oddly neutral-looking faces of the diners, the *maître d'hotel* in his white gloves – bland and uncreased as his own face, the impassive waiters. Everything was perfectly normal; and yet … Some motive he was never after able satisfactorily to explain forced him to let drop into the yawning silence:

'What a marvellous setting this would be for a murder.'

If Nigel had been looking in the right direction at that moment, things might have happened very differently. As it was, he didn't even notice the way Dale's wine glass suddenly tilted and spilt a few drops of sherry.

At once the whole table buzzed again with conversation. A man three places away on Nigel's right raised his head, which had been almost buried in his soup plate, and said:

'Tchah! This is the one place where a murder would never happen. My respected colleagues are men of peace. I doubt if any of them has the guts to say boo to a goose. Oh, yes, they'd *like* to be men of action, tough guys. But, I ask you, just look at them! That's why they became detective writers. Wish fulfilment, the psychoanalysts call it – though I don't give much for that gang, either. But it's quite safe, spilling blood, as long as you only do it on paper.'

The man turned his thick lips and small, arrogant eyes towards Nigel. 'The trouble with you amateur investigators is that you're so romantic. That's why the police beat you to it every time.'

A thick-set, swarthy man opposite him exclaimed: 'You're wrong there, Mr Carruthers. We don't seem to have beaten Mr Strangeways to it in the past every time.'

'So our aggressive friend is *the* David Carruthers. Well, well,' whispered Nigel to Dale.

'Yes,' said Dale, not modifying his tone at all. 'A squalid fellow, isn't he? But he gets the public all right. We have sold our thousands, but David has sold his tens of thousands. Got a yellow streak though, I'll bet, in spite of his bluster. Pity somebody doesn't bump him off at this dinner, just to show him he's not the infallible Pope he sets up to be.'

Carruthers shot a vicious glance at Dale. 'Why not try it yourself? Get you a bit of notoriety, anyway; might even sell your books. Though,' he continued, clapping on the shoulder a nondescript little man who was sitting between him and Dale, 'I think little Crippen here would be my first bet. You'd like to have my blood, Crippen, wouldn't you?'

The little man said stiffly: 'Don't make yourself ridiculous, Carruthers. You must be drunk already. And I'd thank you to remember that my name is Cripps.'

At this point the president interposed with a convulsive change of subject, and the dinner resumed its even tenor. While they were disposing of some very tolerable trout, a waiter informed Dale that he was wanted on the telephone. The young man went out. Nigel was trying at the same time to listen to a highly involved story of the president's and decipher the very curious expression on Cripps's face, when all the lights went out too ...

There were a few seconds of astonished silence. Then a

torrent of talk broke out – the kind of forced jocularity with which man still comforts himself in the face of sudden darkness. Nigel could hear movement all round him, the pushing-back of chairs, quick, muffled treads on the carpet – waiters, no doubt. Someone at the end of the table, rather ridiculously, struck a match; it did nothing but emphasise the pitch-blackness.

'Stevens, can't someone light the candles?' exclaimed the president irritably.

'Excuse me, sir,' came the voice of the *maître d'hôtel*, 'there are no candles. Harry, run along to the fuse-box and find out what's gone wrong.'

The door banged behind the waiter. Less than a minute later the lights all blazed on again. Blinking, like swimmers come up from a deep dive, the diners looked at each other. Nigel observed that Carruthers's face was even nearer his food than usual. Curious, to go on eating all the time. – But no, his head was right on top of the food – lying in the plate like John the Baptist's. And from between his shoulder-blades there stood out a big white handle; the handle – good God! It couldn't be; this was too macabre altogether – but it *was* – the handle of a fish-slice.

A kind of gobbling noise came out of Justice Pottinger's mouth. All eyes turned to where his shaking hand pointed, grew wide with horror and then turned ludicrously back to him, as though he was about to direct the jury.

'God bless my soul!' was all the Judge could say.

But someone had sized up the whole situation. The thick-set man who had been sitting opposite Carruthers was already standing with his back to the door. His voice snapped:

'Stay where you are, everyone. I'm afraid there's no doubt about this. I must take charge of this case at once. Mr Strangeways, will you go and ring up Scotland Yard – police surgeon, fingerprint men, photographers – the whole bag of tricks; you know what we want.'

Nigel sprang up. His gaze, roving round the room, had registered something different, some detail missing; but his mind couldn't identify it. Well, perhaps it would come to him later. He moved towards the door. And just then the door opened brusquey, pushing the thick-set man away from it. There was a general gasp, as though everyone expected to see something walk in with blood on its hands. It was only young Dale, a little white in the face, but grinning amiably.

'What on earth –?' he began. Then he, too, saw …

An hour later, Nigel and the thick-set man, Superintendent Bateman, were alone in the ante-room. The princes of detective fiction were huddled together in another room, talking in shocked whispers.

'Don't like the real thing, do they, sir?' the Superintendent had commented sardonically; 'do 'em good to be up against a flesh-and-blood problem for once. I wish 'em luck with it.'

'Well,' he was saying now. 'Doesn't seem like much of a loss to the world, this Carruthers. None of 'em got a good word for him. Too much food, too much drink, too many women. But that doesn't give us a motive. Now, this Cripps. Carruthers said Cripps would like to have his blood. Why was that, d'you suppose?'

'You can search me. Cripps wasn't giving anything away when we interviewed him.'

'He had enough opportunity. All he had to do when the lights went out was to step over to the buffet, take up the first knife he laid hands on – probably thought the fish-slice was a carving-knife – stab him and sit down and twiddle his fingers.'

'Yes, he could have wrapped his handkerchief round the handle. That would account for there being no finger-prints. And there's no one to swear he moved from his seat; Dale was out of the room – and it's a bit late now to ask Carruthers, who was on his other side. But, if he *did* do it, everything happened very luckily for him.'

'Then there's young Dale himself,' said Bateman, biting the side of his thumb. 'Talked a lot of hot air about bumping Carruthers off before it happened. Might be a double bluff. You see, Mr Strangeways, there's no doubt about that waiter's evidence. The main switch was thrown over. Now, what about this? Dale arranges to be called up during dinner; answers call; then goes and turns off the main switch – in gloves, I suppose, because there's only the waiter's finger-prints on it – comes back under cover of darkness, stabs his man and goes out again.'

'Mm,' ruminated Nigel, 'but the motive? And where are the gloves? And why, if it was premeditated, such an out-landish weapon?'

'If he's hidden the gloves, we'll find 'em soon enough. And – ' the Superintendent was interrupted by the tinkle of the telephone at his elbow. A brief dialogue ensued. Then he turned to Nigel.

'Man I sent round to interview Morton – bloke who rang Dale up at dinner. Swears he was talking to Dale for three to five minutes. That seems to let Dale out, unless it was collusion.'

That moment a plain-clothes man entered, a grin of ill-concealed triumph on his face. He handed a rolled-up pair of black kid gloves to Bateman. 'Tucked away behind the pipes in the lavatories, sir.'

Bateman unrolled them. There were stains on the fingers. He glanced inside the wrists, then passed the gloves to Nigel, pointing at some initials stamped there.

'Well, well,' said Nigel. 'H. D. Let's have him in again. Looks as if that telephone call *was* collusion.'

'Yes, we've got him now.'

But when the young man entered and saw the gloves lying on the table his reactions were very different from what the Superintendent had expected. An expression of relief, instead of the spasm of guilt, passed over his face.

'Stupid of me,' he said, 'I lost my head for a few minutes, after – But I'd better start at the beginning. Carruthers was always bragging about his nerve and the tight corners he'd been in and so on. A poisonous specimen. So Morton and I decided to play a practical joke on him. He was to phone me up; I was to go out and throw the main switch, then come back and pretend to strangle Carruthers from behind – just give him a thorough shaking-up – and leave a blood-curdling message on his plate to the effect that this was just a warning, and next time the Unknown would do the thing properly. We reckoned he'd be gibbering with fright when I turned up the lights again! Well, everything went all right till I came up behind him; but then – then I happened to touch that knife, and I knew somebody had been there before me, in earnest. Afraid, I lost my nerve then, especially when I found I'd got some of his blood on my gloves. So I hid them, and burnt the spoof message. Damn silly of me. The whole idea was damn silly, I can see that now.'

'Why gloves at all?' asked Nigel.

'Well, they say it's your hands and your shirt-front that are likely to show in the dark; so I put on black gloves and pinned my coat over my shirt-front. And, I say,' he added in a deprecating way, 'I don't want to teach you fellows your business, but if I had really meant to kill him, would I have worn gloves with my initials on them?'

'That is as may be,' said Bateman coldly, 'but I must warn you that you are in – '

'Just a minute,' Nigel interrupted. 'Why should Cripps have wanted Carruthers's blood?'

'Oh, you'd better ask Cripps. If he won't tell you, I don't think I ought to – '

'Don't be a fool. You're in a damned tight place, and you can't afford to be chivalrous.'

'Very well. Little Cripps may be dim, but he's a good sort. He told me once, in confidence, that Carruthers had pirated an idea of his for a plot and made a best-seller out of it. A rotten thing to do. But – dash it – no one would commit murder just because –'

'You must leave that for us to decide, Mr Dale,' said the Superintendent.

When the young man had gone out, under the close sur-veillance of a constable, Bateman turned wearily to Nigel.

'Well,' he said, 'it may be him; and it may be Cripps. But, with all these crime authors about, it might be any of 'em.'

Nigel leapt up from his seat. 'Yes,' he exclaimed, 'and that's why we've not thought of anyone else. And' – his eyes lit up – 'by Jove! now I've remembered it – the missing detail. Quick! Are all those waiters and chaps still there?'

'Yes; we've kept 'em in the dining-room. But what the – ?'

Nigel ran into the dining-room, Bateman at his heels. He looked out of one of the windows, open at the top.

'What's down below there?' he asked the *maître d'hôtel*.

'A yard, sir; the kitchen windows look out on it.'

'And now, where was Sir Eldred Travers sitting?'

The man pointed to the place without hesitation, his imperturbable face betraying not the least surprise.

'Right, will you go and ask him to step this way for a minute? Oh, by the way,' he added, as the *maître d'hôtel* reached the door, *'where are your gloves?'*

The man's eyes flickered. 'My gloves, sir?'

'Yes; before the lights went out you were wearing white gloves; after they went up again, I remembered it just now, you were not wearing them. Are they in the yard by any chance?'

The man shot a desperate glance around him; then the bland composure of his face broke up. He collapsed, sobbing, into a chair.

'My daughter – he ruined her – she killed herself. When the lights went out, it was too much for me – the opportunity. He deserved it. I'm not sorry.'

'Yes,' said Nigel, ten minutes later, 'it was too much for him. He picked up the first weapon to hand. Afterwards, knowing everyone would be searched, he had to throw the gloves out of the window. There would be blood on them. With luck, we mightn't have looked in the yard before he could get out to remove them. And, unless one was looking, one wouldn't see them against the snow. They were white.'

'What was that about Sir Eldred Travers?' asked the Superintendent.

'Oh, I wanted to put him off his guard, and to get him away from the window. He might have tried to follow his gloves.'

'Well, that fish-slice might have been a slice of bad luck for young Dale if you hadn't been here,' said the Superintendent, venturing on a witticism. 'What are you grinning away to yourself about?'

'I was just thinking, this must be the first time a Judge has been present at a murder.'

The Ascham

Michael Innes

'I won't swear,' Appleby said, 'that we haven't been mildly rash. But we'll get through.' He changed gear cautiously. *'With luck,* we'll get through … Damn!'

The exclamation was fair enough. The car had been doing splendidly. At times, indeed, it seemed to float on the snow rather than cut through it, and when this happened it showed itself disconcertingly susceptible to the polar attractions – polar in every sense – of the bank rising steeply on its left and the almost obliterated ditch on its right. And now Appleby, steering an uncertain course round a bend, had been obliged to pull up – and to pull up more abruptly than was altogether safe. There was a stationary car straight in front, blocking the narrow road.

'Bother!' Lady Appleby said. 'It's stuck. We'll have to help to dig it out.'

Appleby peered through the windscreen. Snow was still lightly falling through the gathering dusk.

'It won't be a question of helping,' he said. 'If you ask me, it's abandoned. I'll investigate.' He climbed out of the car, and found himself at once up to the knees in snow. 'We've been pretty crazy,' he said, and plunged towards the other car.

Judith Appleby waited for a minute. Then, growing impatient, she climbed out too. She found her husband gazing in some perplexity at the stranded vehicle. It was an ancient but powerful-looking saloon.

'Abandoned, all right,' Appleby said, and tried one of the doors. 'Locked, too. Not helpful, that.'

'What do you mean, not helpful?'

'If we could get in, we could let the brake off, and perhaps be able to shove it aside. It's not all that snowed up, is it?'

'Definitely not.' Judith peered at the wheels. 'Engine failure, perhaps. But it stymies us.'

'Exactly. The driver got away while the going was good. Rather a faint-hearted bolt. And some time ago. There are footprints going on down the road. They've a good deal of fresh snow in them.'

'I suppose that must be called a professional observation. Let's get back into the car. I'm cold. But why didn't the silly ass stay put? It's the safest thing to do. And one can be perfectly snug in a stranded car.' She had kicked some of the snow from her feet and climbed back into her seat. She closed the door beside her. 'It's beautifully warm. Stupid of him to stagger off into the night.'

'Yes, wasn't it?' Appleby climbed in beside his wife. Their

car was rather far from being a conveyance of the most modest order; the abandoned car was markedly humbler and less commodious. Appleby refrained from pointing this out. 'I do find it a shade puzzling,' he said. 'But our own course is fairly simple. We'll reverse as far as those last crossroads. It can't be more than a mile ... Good Lord, what's that?'

'I rather think – ' Turning in her seat, Judith looked through the rear window. 'Yes. It's something sublimely simple, John dear. An avalanche.'

Appleby looked too. 'Avalanche' was perhaps rather a grand word for what had happened. But there could be no doubt about the fact. The bank behind them was extremely steep; nevertheless a surprising depth of snow had contrived to gather on it; and this had now precipitated itself upon the road. Appleby had to waste little time estimating the dimensions of the resulting problem. Their car was trapped.

'Never mind, darling.' Judith, when cross, usually adopted a philosophical tone. 'There's some chocolate in the glove box. And we can keep the engine running and the heater on. It's a good thing you filled up.'

'A good thing *I* filled up? You said – ' Appleby broke off, having glanced at the petrol gauge. It was not one of those occasions upon which expostulation serves any useful purpose. 'There's under a gallon,' he said. 'And we haven't got a spare tin. Civilisation is always lulling one into a false sense of security.'

'But, surely, that's all right? Just ticking over, the petrol will last, won't it, for hours and hours?'

'Undoubtedly. Into the small hours, in fact.'

'The small hours?'

'Two in the morning. Perhaps three.'

'I see.' Judith, who had been contentedly breaking up a slab of chocolate, seemed a little to lose heart. 'John, when the heater stops, how long will the car take to ... to get rather cold?'

'Oh, a quite surprisingly long time. Fifteen minutes. Perhaps even twenty.' Appleby picked up a piece of chocolate. 'I think,' he said rather grimly, 'you'd better get out the map. And I'll turn on this inside light. It's getting dark.'

'We *are* a surprisingly long way from the high road,' Judith said presently. 'I'd no idea.'

'Um,' Appleby said.

'There's that last signpost. At least I think it is.'

'It's a reasonable conjecture.'

'I'd forgotten it was so deserted a countryside. There doesn't seem to be a hamlet, or a house, for miles. But wait a minute.' Judith's finger moved across the map. 'Here's something. "Gore Castle". Only it's in a funny sort of print.'

'That means it's a ruin. They use a Gothic type for places of archaeological or antiquarian interest.'

'But I don't think Gore Castle *is* a ruin – or not all of it. I'm sure I've heard about it.' Judith seemed for the moment to have forgotten their depressed situation. 'Get out the *Historic Houses*.' Appleby did as he was told. The work was very much Judith's vade-mecum, and she flicked through its pages expertly. 'Here we are,' she said. 'Yes, I was quite right. Listen. "Three miles south of Gore. Residence of J. L. Darien-Gore Esq. Dates partly from the thirteenth century. Pictures, tapestry, furniture, stained glass, long gallery – ".'

'I never heard of a medieval castle with a long gallery.'

'It must be the kind of castle that turns into a Jacobean mansion at the back. But let me go on. – "long gallery, formal gardens, famous well".'

'Famous what?'

'Well. A wishing-well, perhaps, or something like that. "April 1 to October 15 – Thursdays only, 2–6. Admission 15p. Tea and biscuits at Castle. Catering facilities at Gore Arms, Gore." I knew I was right.'

'About the biscuits?'

'About its being inhabited. This Darien-Gore person – and I'm sure I've heard the name – '

'It does seem to recall something.'

'Well, he certainly lives there. We've only got to find the place and introduce ourselves.'

'I'd say we only have to find the place. No need to put on a social turn. The chap can't very well thrust us back into the night. Not that the question is other than academic. We can't possibly set out to find Gore Castle. It's almost dark already, and we'd be off the road in no time. That mightn't be a joke. The drifts must be pretty formidable.'

'But, John, I can see the castle. It's positively beckoning to us.'

'*See* it? You're imagining things. Visibility's presently going to be nil.'

'Over there to the right. Let your eye travel past the back of the stranded car. You see?'

'Yes – I see. But –'

'J. L. Darien-Gore Esq. has turned on a light – perhaps high in the keep, or something. It's rather romantic.'

'If it's high in the keep, it may be anything up to five miles away.'

'We can follow it for five miles.'

'My dear Judith, have some sense. Darien-Gore – if it is he – may turn the thing off again at any moment. We're able to see it at all only because it has stopped snowing – '

'Which is encouraging in itself.'

Appleby had produced a small pair of binoculars, and was focusing them on the light.

'I think it possibly is the castle,' he said, and slipped the binoculars back into his coat pocket. 'But we mightn't have gone a hundred yards before we lost it for good, owing to some configuration in the terrain.'

'Bother the terrain. And I'd say we can each carry a suitcase.'

'Dash it all!' Very incautiously, Appleby allowed himself to be diverted by this manoeuvre. 'We can't turn up on the fellow's doorstep as if he ran a blessed hotel!'

'I think it would be only considerate. Otherwise Mr Darien-Gore would have to send grooms and people to rescue our possessions.'

'Sometimes I think you are beginning to suffer from delusions of grandeur.' But Appleby was fishing the suitcases from the back of the car. He'd taken another careful look at that light, and decided it couldn't be very far away. The venture was worth risking. 'At least we've got a torch,' he said. 'So come on.'

They plunged into the snow. But Appleby paused again by the abandoned car. If the fellow had just contrived to steer into the side of the road, they themselves would probably have managed to get past the obstruction, and so be on their way by now. Appleby felt the radiator. He looked again at the surface of the road immediately in front. The snow was thick enough. But it wasn't as thick as all that. He shook his head, and trudged on.

II

'Not at all,' Mr Darien-Gore said. 'The gain is all mine – and my guests. Most delighted to have you here.'

Jasper Darien-Gore was in early middle age. Spare and upright, he would have suggested chiefly an athlete who has carefully kept his form – if he hadn't more obviously and immediately impressed himself as the product of centuries of breeding. His appearance was as thoroughly Anglo-Norman as that of his castle. And he had the air of courteous informality and perfect diffidence – Appleby thought – that masks the arrogance of his kind.

'And I do hope,' Darien-Gore added, 'that this will prove a reasonably comfortable room.'

Appleby looked around him in decent appreciation. It was at least a rather more than reasonably splendid room. If it was comfortable as well – which seemed very likely – this hadn't been secured at the expense of disturbing the general medieval effect. The walls were hung with tapestries in which sundry allegorical events dimly transacted themselves; logs crackled in a fireplace in which it would have been possible to park a small car; there was an enormous four-poster bed. It was no doubt one of the apartments one could view (on Thursdays only) for half-a-crown. Appleby wasn't without an awkward feeling that he ought to produce a couple of half-crowns now.

'Ah!' Darien-Gore said. 'Here is my brother Robert. He has heard of the accession to our company, and has come to add his welcome to mine.'

It seemed to Appleby that these last words had been uttered less by way of politeness than of instruction. Robert Darien-Gore was not looking very adequately welcoming. He was much younger than Jasper, equally handsome, equally athletic in suggestion and decidedly colder and more reserved. Heredity, perhaps, had dealt less kindly with him. His, in fact, was a curiously haunted face – and not the less so from its air of now quickly assuming an appropriate social mask.

'Robert,' Jasper said, 'let me introduce you to –' He broke off. 'By the way, I think it is *Lady* Appleby? But of course. I was sure I recognised your husband. One never knows whether it is quite civil to tell people one has spotted them from photographs in the public prints. Robert – Sir John and Lady Appleby. Sir John is Commissioner of Metropolitan Police.'

'How do you do. I'm so glad you found your way to Gore. It might have been awkward for you, otherwise.' Robert was producing adequate interest. It couldn't have been put higher than that.

'We couldn't possibly have been luckier,' Judith said. 'We had a guidebook, you know. And it said "Tea and biscuits at Castle". I had a wonderful feeling that we were saved.'

'And so you are, Lady Appleby.' Jasper Darien-Gore, who appeared to be more amused than his brother, nodded cordially. 'The kettle, I assure you, is just on the boil.'

Judith, Appleby thought, was made to take this sort of

situation in her stride. One couldn't even say that she was putting on a social turn. She was just being natural. Judith, in fact, ought to have married not a policeman but an ambassador.

'I hope that being held up for a night isn't desperately inconvenient,' Robert said. 'And I really came in to ask at once whether we could do anything about a message. The snow has brought our telephone line down, unfortunately – and it's the same, it seems, at the home farm. But I think we might manage to get one of the men through to the village.'

'Thank you,' Appleby said. 'But there's no need for anything of the sort. Nobody's going to miss us tonight, and I'm sure we can get ourselves dug out in the morning.'

'Then, for the moment, I'll leave you.' Robert turned to his brother. 'They're amusing themselves in the gallery again. I'll just go and see they do nothing lethal.' With the ghost of a smile, he left the room.

'*Thank* you!' Judith was saying – not to her host, but to her host's butler, whose name appeared to be Frape. The fact that Frape himself had brought up their suitcases was a simple index of the grip Judith was getting on the place. '*There*, please.' Judith had pointed to an enormous expanse of oak – it might have been a refectory table of an antiquity not commonly come by – upon which the suitcases would modestly repose. She turned to Darien-Gore. 'It's so stout of you,' she said. 'Sheer pests hammer at your door, frost-bitten and *famished*' – Judith quite shamelessly emphasised this word – 'and you don't bat an eyelid.'

'I had no impulse to bat.' Darien-Gore was amused. 'And, of course, one mustn't – not on one's own doorstep. But, come to think of it, I almost did – bat, I mean – shortly before you came. You see, somebody else has turned up: a fellow who had to abandon a car – '

'The car that prevented ours from getting through, I expect,' Appleby said.

'That may well be. And a perfectly decent fellow, I imagine. Yet I had an obscure impulse to get rid of him – or at least to murmur that Frape would fix him up comfortably – '

'I should be very willing to, sir.' Frape, who had been giving a little ritual attention to the appointments of the room, interrupted his employer. 'And it's not, I think, too late. Nothing very definite has been proposed.'

'Thank you, Frape – but I think not.' Darien-Gore had spoken a shade sharply, and now he waited until the butler had withdrawn. 'Frape finds the fellow not quite qualified to sit on the dais, as one might say. No doubt he's right. But of course he'll dine with us. Under the circumstances, anything else wouldn't be the hospitable thing. Perhaps I was put off when he told me his name was Jolly. Difficult name to live up to – particularly, of course, when your car has been stranded in the snow.'

'I wasn't terribly clear that his car *was* stranded,' Appleby said. 'He didn't say anything to suggest it had broken down?'

'I don't recall that he did. Oh, by the way.' Darien-Gore, who had appeared to be about to take his leave, now changed his mind, and walked over to a heavily curtained window. 'I'm terribly sorry that, in the morning, you won't find much of a view. This room simply looks out on the inner bailey – an enclosed courtyard, that's to say. Perhaps you can see it now. The sky's cleared a little, and there's a moon.' He drew back the curtain. 'Step into the embrasure, and we'll draw these things to again. No need to turn out the lights.'

Appleby and Judith did as they were told. The effect was suddenly to enclose them in a small darkened room, one side of which was almost entirely glass. And as a moon had certainly appeared, they were looking out on a nocturnal scene very adequately illuminated for purposes of picturesque effect. Directly in front of them, the keep of the castle was silhouetted as a dark mass – partly against the sky and partly against the surrounding snows. It was a bleakly rectangular structure, at present encased in a criss-cross of metal and wooden scaffolding. This added to its grim appearance. It was like a prison that had been thrust inside a cage.

'You seem to have quite a job of work on hand, over there,' Appleby said.

'Perfectly true. The weather has halted it for a time, but during the autumn we had masons all over the Castle. The Office of Works pays for most of it, I'm thankful to say.' Darien-Gore laughed whimsically. 'Odd, isn't it? My ancestors built the place to defy the Crown, more or less. And now the Crown comes along, tells me I'm an Ancient Monument and spends pots of money propping up my ruins.'

'Is that the famous well?' Judith asked. She pointed downwards. The inner bailey was a virgin rectangle of untrodden snow – part in shadow and part glittering in the moonlight. In the centre of it a low circular wall, about the size of a large cartwheel, surrounded a patch of impenetrable darkness.

'Yes, that's the well. I see you must really have been reading that guidebook, Lady Appleby. It's certainly what everybody wants to see. We put a grid over it when the castle's being shown – otherwise we might have a nasty bill for damages one day.'

'But why is it famous?' Judith asked. 'Is there some legend connected with it?'

'Nothing of that kind. What's out-of-the-way about it is matter of sober fact. It oughtn't really to be called a well. Think of it as a shaft – an uncommonly deep one – going down to a subterranean river, and you get the idea of it. The guide recites "Kubla Khan" to them, you know. To the tourists, I mean.'

'How very strange!' Judith said. 'Where Alph the sacred river ran?'

'Exactly. And through caverns measureless to man. There's some vast underground system there in the limestone. Ever been to those caves outside Rheims, where you walk for miles between bottles of champagne? It's said to be like that here – only on a vastly larger scale. And, of course, no champagne.'

'Can it be explored?' Judith asked. 'By the kind of people who go pot-holing – that sort of thing?'

'Not possible, it seems. Cast anything down my well, and it's gone for ever. And that doesn't apply merely to orange peel and threepenny bits. If you wanted to get rid of an elephant, and no questions asked or askable, the well would be just the place. It's had its grim enough uses in the past, as you can guess.' Rather abruptly, yet with a touch of achieved showmanship, Darien-Gore closed the curtains. 'We dine at eight,' he said. 'Before that, people often gather for an hour or so in the gallery. At this time of year, it serves its original purpose very well. All sorts of games are possible, and we even manage a little archery. I don't know whether either of you happens to be interested in that sort of thing.'

'I've tried archery from time to time,' Judith said. 'And I'd like to improve.'

'Then you must have a go under Robert's instruction. He's quite keen, I'm glad to say.' Darien-Gore paused, as if uncertain whether to proceed. 'As my small house party consists of intimates, perhaps you will forgive me if I say something more about my brother. He is moody at times. In fact his nervous health has not been good over the past year, and allowances must sometimes be made for him. I think you will like his wife, Prunella. She's a courageous woman.'

'And who else is staying at the Castle?' Judith asked. She had received with the appropriate mild concern the confidence just imparted to her.

'Well, there's Mr Jolly, whom you've heard about. By the way, we've put him in the room next to yours. My glimpse of him doesn't suggest that he will be quite as entertaining as he sounds. Then there's my very old friend Ned Strickland and his wife, Molly – '

'How nice!' Judith said. 'We know them quite well.'

'That's capital – and shows, my dear Lady Appleby, how well house parties arrange themselves at Gore. The only other guest is a fellow called Charles Trevor, who does something or other in the City. We were at school together, and have been trying out a revived acquaintance. And now I'll leave you. The bells do ring, by the way – and just at present there even appear to be young women who answer them. But I don't know what my father would have thought of running Gore on a gaggle of housemaids.'

'A gaggle of housemaids.' Appleby was opening his suitcase with an expression of some gloom. 'I suppose one might call that rather a territorial joke. Would you say I'd better put on this damned dinner jacket?'

'Yes, of course. And it's lucky I brought a decent frock.'

'Our fellow waif-and-stray, Mr Jolly, won't have a dinner jacket.'

'You'll find that one or another of the Darien-Gores will keep him company by not dressing. But the other men will.'

'Oh, very well.' Appleby had little doubt that it would turn out just as Judith said.

'We're lucky to have hit upon such civilised people. And I look forward to seeing the Stricklands.'

'My dear Judith, General Strickland is an amiable bore.'

'Yes – but he's a very old friend of the family. Get him in a corner, and he'll tell you all about the Darien-Gores. I'm curious about them.'

'I'm sure you are. But I doubt whether, there's a great deal to learn. I've a notion that Jasper was once a distinguished athlete – '

'Yes, that rings a bell. Something aquatic – high diving or water polo or – '

'No doubt. And he's simply lived on his rents ever since. As for the melancholic Robert, perhaps the less one learns the better.'

'Just what do you mean by that?' Having found the dress she wanted, Judith was shaking it out on its hanger. 'You don't think he's mad, do you?'

'I'd hardly suppose so. But when a chap like Jasper

Darien-Gore starts apologising for his brother in advance, one has to suppose there's something rather far wrong. And I've an impression that Robert, and presumably his wife, Prunella, aren't simply here on a weekend visit. In some obscure way, Robert has taken refuge here. And you and I, my dear, butting in in the way we have butted in, have very precisely the social duty to discover nothing about it.'

'Perhaps we have. Only it's not in your nature, John, to refrain from looking into things – just as you're doing now.'

This was fair enough. Turning out his pockets as he changed, Appleby had come upon the binoculars he had first used in search of Gore Castle. He had drawn back a curtain and was using them now to take a closer look at the inner bailey. The moon was rising, and the sky had blown clear. Straight opposite, the keep was no longer a mere dark mass within its scaffolding. One could make out something of the detail of its surface, pierced by narrow unglazed windows. Below, the carpet of snow, untrodden even by the tracks of cat or bird, surrounded the sinister well.

'Come along,' Judith said. 'We mustn't skulk.'

Appleby closed the curtain and put down the binoculars. They left the room together. A few paces down the corridor, there was a half-open door on their right. And it was true that Appleby could seldom refrain from looking into things. He did so now. A middle-aged man, sharp-featured and indefinably furtive, appeared to have turned back into the room when about to leave it. He was now transferring from a small suitcase to a jacket pocket what appeared to be a rather bulky pocketbook.

'Well, well!' Appleby had walked on for some paces before

he murmured this. 'Not only do we know the Stricklands. We know Mr Jolly as well.'

'Nonsense! I took a glance at the man. I'm certain I've never seen him before.'

'All right. But *I* know Mr Jolly quite well. Possibly he doesn't know me.'

'I don't see how –'

'I know him by sight, I ought to say. I've had the advantage of studying his photograph.'

'You mean he's a criminal?'

'He's thought to be. Perhaps it wouldn't be fair to put it stronger than that.'

'Then he's in for a fright when he discovers who you are.'

'I suppose he's bound to do that. Yes, I suppose Darien-Gore is bound to tell him.'

'Hadn't *you* better tell Darien-Gore – I mean, that he's sheltering somebody who may be after the family silver?'

'Perhaps so.' Appleby frowned. 'Only, it mightn't be altogether tactful. You see, Mr Jolly's line happens to be blackmail.'

'How revolting! But surely –'

'I think,' Appleby said, 'we go up this staircase to reach the famous long gallery.'

III

'One moment, my lady, if you please.' Frape had stepped forward rather dramatically out of shadow. 'You would find it safer to come up by the staircase at the other end of the gallery.'

'You mean that this one may tumble down?' Judith looked in some alarm behind her. It had been a stiff climb.

'Nothing of that kind, my lady. But to enter the gallery by this door – ' Frape broke off as a sharp twang made itself heard from the direction in which he was pointing. 'That would be Mr Robert,' he said. 'Or it might be Mr Charles Trevor. Both draw a powerful bow. If that indeed be the correct expression among archers … Ah!' The twang had made itself heard again.

'I think I see what you mean,' Appleby said. 'It wouldn't be healthy to get in the way of *that.*'

'Precisely, sir. But in a moment the round – if they call it that – will be over. You and her ladyship can then enter. Meanwhile, sir, may I ask if you have seen anything of Mr Jolly?'

'Yes – and I imagine he's coming along.'

'I am glad to hear it, sir. It had occurred to me that he might be lingering awkwardly in his room.' Frape turned to Judith. It was clear that he regarded her as worthier of the august confidence of an upper servant than was her husband. 'To my mind,' he murmured, 'an error of judgement on Mr Robert's part. Persons are best accommodated according to their evident station. Mr Jolly would have done very well in the servants' hall. And I could have answered for it that there would be no complaints.'

'I'm sure there wouldn't,' Judith said.

'Precisely, my lady. My own service has always been in large establishments and among the old gentry. In such circumstances one becomes accustomed to entertaining odd visitors from time to time. Even chauffeurs are occasionally odd. And ladies' maids, I am sorry to say, are becoming increasingly so – as your ladyship is doubtless aware.'

'I haven't had one since I came out. So I wouldn't know.' Judith spoke with a briskness that doubtless characterised – Appleby thought – the old gentry rather than the new. But now, from beyond the door over which the communicative Frape stood guard, there came a small sound as of polite applause. 'They must have finished the end.'

'The end, my lady?'

'It's called an end, Mr Frape, not a round.'

Appleby, who would have addressed Frape as Frape, and who knew nothing about ends, felt that Judith had smartly scored two points at once.

'In other words,' he said, 'we can go in.'

'Exactly so, sir.' And Frape, with a grave bow, opened the door of the long gallery.

'As you'll notice, we manage fifty yards – which is quite a regular ladies' length. And there's plenty of height, as you see.' Prunella Darien-Gore was explaining this to Judith – and with a shade of desperation, Appleby thought. Her husband, who ought to have been giving these explanations, seemed to be sunk in a sombre reverie. 'Mr Trevor, will you show Lady Appleby?'

'Yes, of course.' Charles Trevor was stout and flabby; one would have guessed that he was without either interest or skill in athletic pursuits. But now he slipped on brace and tips, and with a casual certainty sent one arrow into the gold and two into the red. 'Robert?' he said challengingly.

Robert Darien-Gore came out of his abstraction with a start, and picked up his own bow without a word. Appleby, standing beside Robert's wife, was aware of a curious tension in her as she watched. He spoke out of an impulse in some way to relieve this.

'I know nothing about archery,' he said. 'But it's my guess that your husband is pretty good?'

'He used to be.' Prunella, Appleby saw, was digging her nails hard into the palms of her hands. 'It came second only to his rock-climbing.' She gave a suppressed gasp, as if suddenly aware that she was thinking of her husband as somebody out of the past. 'Yes,' she said. 'Robert is first-class. Watch.' Her sudden faith in her husband was justified. Robert shot three arrows and bettered Trevor's score. Into his final shot he appeared to have put unnecessary force. The shaft had buried itself deep in the heart of the target. In the middle ages, Appleby remembered, an arrow from an English long bow could pierce the thickest armour. And there was something alarming in this one. Its feathered tip was still quivering as he watched.

'Capital, my dear Robert!' General Strickland, who had been talking to Jasper Darien-Gore in a corner, set down a glass in order to applaud vigorously. 'Let's see if Trevor can beat that – eh? Just let me retrieve the things.' He turned to Appleby. 'We don't manage two ends, you see. It would lose us five yards we can't spare. So we shoot only from this end. Nobody do anything careless, please!' He hurried off down the length of the gallery.

'Ned isn't in Robert's class,' Mrs Strickland said to Judith. 'Nor in this Mr Trevor's either. But he can give Jasper a good match. I'm very much afraid he may want to now. Aren't you famished, Judith?'

'Quite famished. I suppose we're waiting for Mr Jolly.'

'Mr Jolly – whoever is he?'

'The other gatecrasher. He seems to have made the haven of Gore Castle about an hour before John and I did.'

'How very odd. I hope he isn't keen on archery too. I find it tedious – and a little unnerving.'

'Unnerving, Molly? I suppose it has a lethal background – or history. But – '

'I think it's that terrible twang – like something going wrong with a piano. But here they go again.'

General Strickland had retrieved the arrows, and now Charles Trevor was again addressing himself to the target. He sent his first arrow into the gold.

'There!' Mrs Strickland said. 'Didn't you hear? Like something happening to the poor old family Bechstein – or perhaps to one's grand-daughter's cello – in the middle of the night. Have you never been wakened up by just that?'

'I have.' Appleby, who had been accepting a drink from Frape, paused beside her. 'But, you know – '

'*Stop!*'

It was the vigilant Frape who had given this shout. And he was only just in time. As Trevor drew back the bowstring the door at the farther end of the gallery had opened, and Jolly had walked in. Not unnaturally, he stood transfixed, staring up the gallery at Trevor. And, for an alarming moment, Trevor himself oddly swayed, and with a queer and involuntary movement seemed almost to train his arrow upon the newcomer. Then he let his bow gently unflex. There was a moment or two of mild confusion, followed by introductions. These last were not without awkwardness. Jolly seemed indisposed to make any claim upon the social graces.

He gave each of the women in turn what was no doubt meant for a bow, but had more the appearance of a wary cringe. His glance tended to go apprehensively towards Trevor – as it still well might – and then travel furtively towards Robert. Frape stood in the background. It was evident that the proceedings were very far from enjoying his approval.

'Lady Appleby,' Jasper was saying. 'And Sir John Appleby. Sir John is – '

'How do you do?' Without too great an effect of abruptness, Appleby had cut explanations short. 'We're in the same boat, you and I. My car got stranded behind yours. Was it just the snow held you up, or did you have engine trouble?'

'A little bit of one thing and a little bit of another.' Jolly, whose address was no more polished than his manner, eyed Appleby narrowly. 'Acquainted with these people here, are you?' he asked.

'I happen to know General Strickland and his wife. But not the others.'

'I'm a stranger here myself. They invited me to stay the night. Affable, you might say. Not that they could well do anything else. Plenty of room in a place like this.'

'Clearly there is.'

'And no need to stint, either. Money in a big way, eh? And a touch of real class as well. I've a fancy for that. High aristocratic feeling. Sense of honour and so on.' Jolly gestured at the line of family portraits which hung in the long gallery. 'Eyes of one's ancestors upon one, eh? There's something I like about that.'

'No doubt you find it professionally advantageous. By the way, I gather you've met Mr Trevor before?'

'Trevor?' Jolly was startled. 'Who is he? Never heard of him.'

'He's the man who was about to shoot when you came into the gallery. I got the impression that you were looking at each other with some kind of recognition.'

'Nothing of the kind. What I recognised was that he very nearly killed me.'

'I don't know that he did quite that. But it was an awkward moment, certainly. It was natural that he should be agitated – that he should be a little agitated. I think I must go and have a word with him.'

'Does one require a licence,' Appleby asked casually, 'to play around with bows and arrows?'

'Good Lord, no!' Charles Trevor glanced at Appleby in surprise – and also, perhaps, with a faint impression of quick alarm. 'Why ever should one?'

'It has occurred to me that the things are just as efficient weapons as pistols and revolvers – more efficient than some. I've seen that you can put an arrow through the pin-hole – isn't it called? – on that target. I doubt whether you could do the same thing with an automatic.'

'I've never handled a pistol in my life, so that's no doubt true.'

'Ah! Now, suppose that incident a few minutes ago had really resulted in an accident. Suppose you'd fired – or does one say shot? – dead at this fellow Jolly. You'd actually have transfixed him, wouldn't you?'

'Really, my dear sir! I don't know that it's very pleasant to –'

'He'd have been pinned to the wall, like a living butterfly that some cruel child – '

'Dash it all – ' Not unreasonably, Trevor appeared outraged by this macabre before-dinner chat.

'I was only thinking, you know, that if one had sufficient cause really to hate a man, an arrow might be a more attractive weapon than a bullet. But you must forgive me. I'm a policeman, remember. My mind runs on these matters from time to time. And – do you know? – I can almost imagine that some people *would* hate Mr Jolly – quite a lot. I'd say he's a type one rather likes to forget about. Supposing when one *had* forgotten him – '

'I care nothing for this fellow Jolly. And I certainly don't think him worth talking about.'

'I was going to say that when the Jollys of this life *do* bob up again, the desirable thing is probably to keep one's head. As for talking – well, he's at least not a very conversable character himself. Look at him now.'

Jasper and General Strickland were competing against each other, though in rather a casual way. The others were engaged in desultory conversation behind them. Jolly, however, had retired to a window-seat at the side of the gallery. And he began, as Appleby looked, to fumble in a pocket. He might have been hunting for a cigarette case or a box of matches. But what he brought out was a dark, bulky pocketbook. It was familiar to Appleby already. He had seen it, through the open bedroom door, going into Jolly's pocket earlier in the evening. Having produced it, Jolly did nothing more. He simply sat immobile, with the thing in his lap.

Appleby turned back to the others. He was just in time

to catch a swift impression of the Darien-Gore brothers, momentarily immobile, gazing into each other's eyes. Then Jasper drew back his bow-string, and there followed the twang to which Molly Strickland took such exception. The shaft flew wide. There was a moment's silence in the gallery. It was broken by Frape.

'*Dinner is served!*'

IV

'I shall be delighted to have coffee in the gallery,' Mrs Strickland said as she re-entered it. 'I don't know a more charming room. But I make one condition – that those tiresome bows and arrows be put away. Judith, you agree?'

'I think I do. If the men find more talk with us boring, they can go away and play billiards.'

'Prunella, dear, you are hostess.' Mrs Strickland spoke a shade sharply. 'The onus is on you.'

'But of course!' Robert's wife had walked into the room in an abstraction. Now she turned round with a start. 'Only you needn't be anxious, Molly. There's never any archery after dinner. Jasper would as soon think to settle down to talk about money. Everything has been put in the ascham.'

'The what, dear?' The three women were alone, and Mrs Strickland was helping herself to coffee.

'Oh, I'm so sorry.' Prunella had again started out of inattention. 'The ascham is the name given to the cupboard where bows and things are kept. There it is.' She indicated a tall and beautiful piece of furniture, perhaps Elizabethan in period, which stood against the wall. 'I think it must be named after some famous archer.'

'Roger Ascham,' Judith said, a shade instructively. 'He wrote a book called *Toxophilus*. He was a schoolmaster.'

'I am sure he was an excessively dreary person.' Mrs Strickland was studying a row of bottles. 'Why, in bachelor establishments, are women of unblemished reputation invariably confronted with *Crème de Menthe*? Never mind. There's a perfectly respectable brandy too.'

'I am sure there is.' Prunella spoke rather dryly. 'And won't you have a cigar?'

'Only at home, dear. That has always been my rule.'

Judith, too, found herself some brandy. So far, the evening had not been a success, and it appeared unlikely that it would perk up now. Dinner, indeed, had been so constrained an affair that the tactful thing would probably be an acknowledgement of the fact, made upon a whimsical note.

'John and I did our best,' she said. 'But we were foreign bodies, I suppose. It all *didn't* seem to mix terribly well.'

'One must blame that really *sombre* Mr Jolly,' Mrs Strickland said. 'He disappointed me. One so seldom has an opportunity of meeting that sort of person – unless one goes canvassing at election time, or something of that kind. But he *quite* refused to be drawn out.'

'I'm afraid Robert was rather silent.' Prunella was gazing into her untasted cup of coffee. 'But he has been depressed ever since he … he resigned his commission. Jasper is very good – '

'One can see that they are devoted to each other,' Judith said.

'Yes – Jasper wants Robert to take over the running of

the estate. I hope he will. It would be so much better than ...
than simply hanging around.'

There was an awkward silence, resolutely broken by Mrs
Strickland.

'Jasper did his best with us – at dinner, I mean. He can
talk so well about the history of Gore. Of course, I've heard
parts of it before. But he told us some things that were quite
new. About the ghost that walks in this gallery. I'm sure I
never heard of that. Do you think it goes about pierced by
an arrow? I wouldn't be at all surprised. And the superstition
about the well at midnight – '

'There's a superstition about the well?' Judith asked.

'Yes. Didn't you hear? And I'm quite sure that I wouldn't
care – But here are the men. I had a notion they wouldn't
linger very long.'

'A very good dinner,' General Strickland said to Appleby.
The two men were sitting in a corner of the gallery apart. 'A
very good dinner, indeed.'

'It might have been a shade more lively, I thought.'

'Lively? I don't believe in dinners being lively. Not with
a Margaux like that. Chatter spoils one's concentration, if
you ask me.'

'Margaux, was it? Judith said it tasted rather like cowslip
wine.'

'My dear boy, she was perfectly right. She always is.
That's the precise description for the bouquet of Margaux.
Ever been to the Château?' Strickland paused to sniff at his
brandy. 'I must tell you, one day, of the week I spent there in
'17. Absolutely amazing. Not that the place is anything much
to look at. Not a patch on Gore. Built by some fellow called

Lacolonilla about a hundred years ago, and might be round the corner from my own house in Regent's Park … How does Gore strike you, by the way?'

'It's an impressive place – particularly to tumble into out of the snow. And perhaps a shade oppressive, as well.'

'Never struck me that way. But then I've known it, you see, man and boy … Bit of a cloud over it at the moment, eh?'

'So I feel. But Judith and I are unbidden guests, you know. I told her, earlier this evening, that curiosity isn't on.'

'And she said that, with you, it's never off?'

'Well, as a matter of fact, she did.' Appleby paused to light a cigar.

'But, Strickland – do you know? – I'm not sure I wouldn't like any gossip there is. I've a notion there's something … well, building up. Any idea what I mean?'

General Strickland looked about him cautiously. But the two men were unobserved – except by the ancestral Darien-Gore portraits on the walls.

'That fellow Charles Trevor seems deucedly uneasy,' he said. 'And what's he doing here, anyway? Knows his spoons and forks, and all that. In fact, he was at school with Jasper. But not our sort. Not our sort, at all.'

'I suppose not.' Appleby was amused by this obscure social judgement. 'But I imagine he's more our sort than poor Mr Jolly.'

'Well, that's different. Very decent, unassuming chap, no doubt. Some sort of counter-jumper or motor salesman, eh? Jasper didn't want to bother the servants with him.'

'So I've gathered – if it was Jasper. I rather think it may

have been Robert. There's a faint conflict of evidence on the point.'

'Well, it comes to the same thing, my dear boy. The brothers are tremendously thick. And, since Robert and Prunella came to live here – '

'Why did they come?'

'Ah – that's telling.'

'I know.'

'Appleby, you really feel there's something … well, *happening in* this place?'

'Happening, or going to happen. Don't you?'

'That could be stopped?'

'Well, not by me. I just don't know enough.' Appleby paused to look into his brandy glass. 'Were you going to tell me about Robert?'

'My dear chap, *I* don't know. Nobody does – or wants to, I should hope. It looked damnably ugly for a time. And then it ended on what you might call a minor note.'

'Ended? What ended?'

'Robert's career, I suppose one has to say. He left the army. And the thing dropped.'

'The thing? What thing?'

'God knows, something there turned out not to be sufficient evidence about, I imagine.' General Strickland broke off, and again looked about him. This time, it was at the line of portraits silent on the wall. 'A poor show of some sort. Hard on a decent family, eh? Not much wrong with them since the Crusades, and all that.'

'You're a romantic at heart, Strickland. And noblesse oblige is all very well, no doubt.' Appleby was speaking seriously. 'But that particular sense of obligation is an open invitation to pride.'

'And pride?'

'Is an open invitation to the devil.'

'Here's Jasper coming down the gallery. He *looks* proud, I'm bound to admit. But he's ageing, too. It's just struck me. Still, he's kept his form. A great athlete, you know, as a young man. But not the sort that falls into a flabby middle age … I think he's coming over to talk to you. I must go and have another word with your wife. Astonishing thing, you two turning up here like that. Quite astonishing.'

'Delightful that you turned out to know the Stricklands,' Jasper Darien-Gore said. 'Won't you and your wife treat it as an inducement to stay on for a day or two?'

'It's most hospitable of you, but I'm afraid we can't.' Appleby felt no reason to suppose that Darien-Gore had spoken other than merely by way of civility. There was, indeed, something faintly distraught in his manner which emphasised the point. 'As a matter of fact, we must try to get away fairly early.' Appleby hesitated, and then took a plunge. 'Unless, that is, I can be useful in any way.' He waited for a response, but none came. Darien-Gore was looking at him with a frozen and conventional smile. He simply mightn't have heard. Having begun, however, Appleby went on. 'You'll forgive me if I'm talking nonsense. But it has just occurred to me that in that fellow Jolly you may find your-self rather far from entertaining an angel unawares. And I happen to know – '

'Jolly?' Darien-Gore repeated the name quite vaguely.

'An odd chap, I agree. But he has been getting on quite well with Robert. In fact, they've been making some kind of wager – I've no idea about what.'

'I don't think I'd be inclined to lay any wager with Jolly. Winning and losing might prove equally expensive.'

'And he says that he must try to get away quite early, too. Ah, here he is.'

This was not wholly accurate. Jolly had been standing some little way across the. gallery, and without showing any disposition to approach. But Jasper had made a gesture which constrained him to come forward.

'Mr Jolly,' he said, ' – you must really leave us in the morning, if your car can be got away? It would be pleasant if you could stay a little longer.' As he produced this further civility, Jasper gave Appleby a hard smile. 'And, of course –' He broke off. 'Ah – thank you, Frape.'

Frape's appearance was with a large silver tray, upon which he was carrying round a whisky decanter, glasses, ice and a syphon. The Darien-Gores, it was to be supposed, kept fairly early hours. Frape was looking particularly wooden. He had presumably overheard his employer's latest essay in hospitality.

'Very much obliged,' Jolly said. 'But fast and far will be my motto in the morning. All having gone well, that's to say.' He gave a laugh which was at once insolent and apprehensive. 'Yes, all having gone well.' He looked indecisively at the tray – and at this moment Robert Darien-Gore came up. Silently, he poured a stiff drink, added a splash of soda water and handed the glass to Jolly. Jolly, who already seemed slightly drunk, gulped, hesitated, gulped again. The two brothers watched him fixedly. He returned the glass, only half-emptied, to the tray, and waved Frape away. Frape's eyes met Appleby's for a moment, and then he moved silently off.

'I know just when I've been given enough,' Jolly said. 'And it has been the secret of my success.' He turned to Appleby, and gave him a look of startling contempt. 'Pleasant to meet people one has heard about,' he said. 'Isn't that right, Sir John?'

'Decidedly. And I'm glad, Mr Jolly, that I've been here to meet you tonight.'

'I know, you see, just how much I can take.' Jolly pointed at Appleby's glass, as if further to explain this remark. 'That, and fast and far, are the secrets of my success.'

'Come and have a final word with my wife, Mr Jolly.' Quite firmly, Appleby took Jolly by the elbow and led him away – leaving the Darien-Gores looking at each other silently. But Appleby took no more than a few paces towards Judith. 'My man,' he said, 'let me give you a word of advice. Stick, on this occasion, to fast and far. And make it quite clear that you have forgotten the other part of your secret of success.'

'I don't know what you're talking about.'

'I'm talking about life and death. Good night.'

V

'Good night, madam ... good night, sir ... good night, my lady.' Frape, standing at one of the doors of the long gallery, responded to such salutations as he was offered while the company dispersed. His employer and his employer's brother were the last to leave the gallery; to each of the Darien-Gores, as he very slightly bowed, he gave a grave, straight look. Jasper hesitated when at the head of the staircase, half-turned as if about to speak, thought better of it and moved on. Robert had already vanished; in a moment Jasper's shoulders – squarely held – and then his head vanished too. Frape closed the door behind him, turned and looked down the long gallery. From its far end the archery target regarded him like a staring and sleepless eye. He moved down the gallery, set glasses on a tray, placed a guard carefully before the great fireplace, turned off the lights, so that it was now by the flicker of firelight that he was lit, paused to look thoughtfully at the line of portraits on the wall. He went over to the ascham and saw that it was locked. He moved to a window, drew back a curtain and stood immobile before the wintry scene. Small clouds were drifting across a high, full moon, so that pale light and near-blackness washed alternately over the landscape. To his left, and from very high up, he had an oblique view of the inner bailey; this came into full light for a moment, revealing the well, still amid its unbroken carpet of snow.

Frape remained motionless, with the firelight flickering behind him.

VI

'Snubbed,' Appleby said.

'Never mind, darling. This is a most comfortable bed. And do hurry up. I'm extremely sleepy.' Judith put down the book she had been reading. 'You mean you scrapped that business about having a social duty to discover nothing?'

'More or less.' Appleby took off his black tie and tossed it on the dressing-table. 'At least, I decided that I ought to offer our host some sort of warning about Jolly. What I was after was a little candour before trouble blows up.'

'What sort of trouble?'

'Unfortunately, I can't take more than a guess at it. If I could do more, it might be possible to act. Anyway, our friend Jasper refused to play. So did Jolly.'

'Jolly! You talked to him?'

'He's up to mischief, and I had a shot at sharing him off. It didn't work. You'd take him to be rather an apprehensive little rat, but in fact he has a nerve. It amuses him to be operating – and he certainly is operating – right under my nose.'

'He's gathered who you are?'

'Quite clearly he has. But I don't seem to carry around with me much of the terror of the law.'

'There's something between him and that man Charles Trevor.'

'I know there is.' Appleby was now in his pyjamas.

'I think Trevor is quite as nasty as Jolly. Perhaps they're confederates.'

'Perhaps.'

'You say something's going to happen. What?'

'Well, for one thing, you and I are going to sleep.' Appleby turned out a light. 'For another – but this is where I just start to guess – there's going to be some hard bargaining at Gore. And not of a kind, unfortunately, at which I can very well act as honest broker.'

'It sounds most unpleasant.'

'I'm sure it is. But I don't see there is anything I can do. I must think twice before compounding a felony, I suppose. And that's why, in a way, I don't really want to learn more.

We didn't stagger in here out of the snow in order to start blowing police whistles and insisting on open scandal. Or that's how I see it at the moment. It may be different in the morning.' Appleby crossed to the window, drew back the curtain a little way and half-opened a casement. He moved back across the room, got into bed and turned out the last light. The room was quite dark, with only a narrow band of moonlight falling on a wall and across the bed. 'And now you're going straight to sleep,' he said.

The band of moonlight had moved a little; it now caught the corner of a picture. Otherwise the room was in absolute darkness. The only sound was Judith's breathing.

'*Twang!*'

Appleby found that he had come awake with a start, and that his mind was groping for the reason. And the reason came to him, like an echo on the inward ear, as he sat up and switched on a bedside lamp. Judith was still fast asleep.

He picked up his watch and looked at it; the time was just two o'clock. He slipped out of bed, went over to the door and listened intently. He came back, put on his dressing-gown, felt in his open suitcase and produced a pocket torch. Returning to the door, he opened it gently, went out and closed it behind him. The corridor before him was quite dark and very cold. He let the beam from his torch first play down its empty length, and then circle until it found the door of Jolly's room. He went over to this, listened for some seconds and then switched off the torch and cautiously turned the handle. The door swung back with a faint creak upon blackness. He switched on the torch again, and the beam fell on

Jolly's shabby suitcase, open and untidy. The beam circled the room and fell upon the bed. It had been turned down at one corner. But nobody had slept in it.

Appleby closed the door – and as he did so heard faint sounds from the end of the corridor. They might have been slippered footfalls. He turned in time to see a dim form and a flickering light disappear round a corner. Muffling the torch in the skirt of his dressing-gown, he followed.

Under these conditions, Gore Castle seemed tortuous and enormous. Several times he lost all trace of the figure in front of him. And then, suddenly, he oriented himself. The newel by which he was standing belonged to one of the two staircases leading to the long gallery. He looked up. An unidentifiable male figure – like himself, in a dressing-gown, but holding a lighted candle before him – was disappearing into the long gallery itself. Appleby climbed rapidly. The gallery, when he reached it, was part in near-darkness and part floating in moonlight. At its far end stood the target, commanding the long, narrow place. Appleby rounded a screen, and the man with the candle stood before him. It was Frape. His hand was on the door of the ascham.

'What's this about, Frape?'

The candlestick in Frape's hand gave a jump. But when he turned round, it was to look at Appleby steadily enough.

'The door of the ascham, sir. It seems to have been left unsecured, and to have been banging in the night. The fault is mine, sir. I am deeply sorry that you, too, should have been disturbed by it.'

'Nonsense.'

'I beg your pardon, sir?'

'You are talking nonsense, Frape, as you very well know.'

'I assure you, sir – '

'Open the door of the thing, and let's have a look. It's no more than you were going to do for yourself.'

Silently, Frape turned back and opened the door of the tall cupboard.

'Commendable,' Appleby said. 'Everything as accountable as in a well-ordered armoury. Those two empty places in the rack, Frape – I think they mean two arrows missing?'

'It might be so, sir. I cannot tell.'

'Two gone.' Appleby lifted a third arrow from the rack and poised it in his hand. 'Simply as a dagger,' he said, 'it would make a pretty lethal weapon – would it not?'

'I really can't say, sir.'

'But there's a bow missing as well?'

'There may be, sir. I have never counted them, so am not in a position to say.'

'Frape, drop this. It can do nobody any good. You came up here – didn't you? – because you were disturbed by the same sound that disturbed me. Somebody shooting one of those damned things. And we both know that nobody practises archery in the small hours just for fun.'

'There is the possibility of a bet, sir. Gentlemen have their peculiar ways.'

'For heaven's sake, man, stop behaving like a stage butler. You know, even better than I do, that there's some devilry afoot in this place.'

'Yes … yes, I do.' Frape passed a hand over his forehead, like a man who gives up. 'Only, I must – '

At this moment the creak of a door made itself heard

from the far end of the gallery. Appleby was about to turn towards the noise, when Frape restrained him.

'Don't turn round,' he said in a low voice. 'I can see – without being detected as doing so. I think somebody is watching us through the door.' He began to fiddle with the door-handle of the ascham. 'Yes,' he said in a louder tone. 'The catch is defective, sir, and so the door has simply been blowing to and fro. There is always a draught in the gallery.' Once more he lowered his voice. 'He's opened it wider. It's Mr Trevor. He's shut it again. He's gone.'

'You mean to say' – now Appleby did turn round – 'that this fellow Trevor has come up here, peered in at us in a furtive manner and made himself scarce again?'

'Yes, sir. And it is certainly another indication that things are not as they ought to be.'

'Quite so. And the question is, where do we go from here? Have you any idea where we might find that fellow Jolly?'

'In his bed, I suppose.'

'Jolly's bed hasn't been slept in. Were you aware of any coming and going about the place after the company broke up last night?'

'I have an impression, sir, that there was some talking going on in the library until about midnight. Whether Mr Jolly was concerned, I don't know. But would I be correct in assuming that you are aware of something seriously to his disadvantage?'

'That puts it mildly, Frape. The man's a professional criminal.'

'Then I suggest that he may have left the Castle. Mr Darien-Gore may have detected him in some design that has resulted in his beating a hasty retreat. It would be perfectly possible. The wind has dropped, and I think there has been no more snow.' As he said this, and as if to confirm his impression, Frape crossed over to a window.

'It's a possibility, certainly,' Appleby said. 'And I wonder –'

'Sir' – Frape's voice had changed suddenly – 'will you be so good as to step this way?'

Appleby did so, and found himself looking obliquely down into the moonlit inner bailey. It was a moment before he realised the small change that had taken place in the scene. Between the well and one side of the surrounding courtyard there was a line of tracks in the snow.

'Mr Darien-Gore's binoculars, sir. He keeps a pair in the gallery.'

Appleby took the binoculars and focused. There could be no doubt about what he saw. A line of heavy footprints led straight to the well. There were none leading the other way.

'Ought I to rouse Mr Darien-Gore, sir?' Frape asked, as Appleby put down the binoculars and turned away from the window.

'Certainly you must.' Appleby moved across the gallery to the great fireplace. 'And everybody else as well. But it will be rather a chilly occasion for them – particularly for the ladies. Would you say, Frape, that this fire could be blown up quickly?'

'Decidedly, sir. A little work with the bellows will produce a blaze in a few minutes.'

'Then this will be the best place in which to meet. You had better get on to the job ... But one moment.' Appleby held up a hand. 'You could not have been mistaken about the identity of the man peering in on us a few moments ago?'

'Certainly not. It was Mr Trevor.'

'Nor could you have had any motive for ... deceiving me in the matter?'

'I quite fail to understand you, sir.'

'Do you think that Mr Trevor – if Mr Trevor it is – may have some reason for entering the gallery? Might he be outside that door still, hoping that we shall leave by the other one?'

'I can't imagine any reason for such a thing.'

'Can't you? Well, I propose to put it to the test, by going down the one staircase, through the hall and up the other one now. You will stay here, please, blowing up the fire.'

'I don't see that – '

'Frape, you're far from being in the dark about what we're up against. Please do as I say.'

This time, Appleby waited for no reply, but left the gallery by the door beside the target and ran downstairs, playing his torch before him. As an outflanking move it seemed a forlorn hope, but in fact it was startlingly successful. When, a couple of minutes later, he returned breathlessly into the gallery by the other door, he was hustling before him a figure who had in fact still been lurking there. It wasn't Charles Trevor. It was Robert Darien-Gore.

'All right, Frape,' Appleby said. 'Get everybody in here. But give them a few minutes to get dressed – and get dressed yourself.' He turned to Robert, who was wearing knicker-bockers and a shooting jacket. 'You mustn't mind my staying as I am,' he said. 'It might be a mistake if you and I were to waste any time in beginning to work this thing out.'

VII

'Good God!' General Strickland said, and put down the binoculars. He was the last of the company to have accepted Appleby's invitation to scrutinise the inner bailey. 'The fellow walked deliberately out and killed himself. And in that hideous way.'

'It isn't,' Mrs Strickland asked, 'some ... some abominable joke? He can't, for instance, have tiptoed back again in his own prints in the snow?'

'I'm afraid not.' Appleby, who was planted before what was now a brisk fire, shook his head. 'Robert Darien-Gore was good enough to accompany me down to the inner bailey a few minutes ago. We didn't go right out to the well – I want those tracks photographed before any others are made – but I satisfied myself – professionally, if I may so express it – that nobody can have come back through that snow. Whatever the tracks tell, they don't tell that.'

'The snow on the parapet,' Trevor said rather hoarsely, '– on the low wall, I mean, round the well – seems to have prints at one point too.'

'Precisely. And the picture seems very clear. There is one person, and one person only, missing from the castle now – a chance guest like myself: the man Jolly. Whether deliberately or by accident, he has ... gone down the well. And I believe you all know what *that* means.'

'By accident?' Strickland asked. 'How could it be an accident?'

'I can't see how it could possibly be,' Judith Appleby said. 'No sane man would take it into his head to go out in the middle of the night – '

'He was a bit tight,' Jasper Darien-Gore said. 'I don't know if that's relevant, but it's a fact. Frape – you noticed it?'

'Most emphatically, sir. Although not incapacitated, the man was undoubtedly tipsy.'

'He must have decided to go back to his car.' Prunella Darien-Gore broke in with this. 'He thought he'd go outside the castle, and he went blundering through the snow – '

'It's not impossible,' Appleby said. 'Only it doesn't account for Jolly's climbing up on the lip of the well. Face up to that, and suicide is the only explanation. Or it would seem to be. But Mr Robert has another theory. You may judge it bizarre, but it fits the facts. Frape, do you remember saying something to me about a bet?'

'Yes, sir. It was in a slightly different connection. But the point is a very relevant one.'

'And I think you remarked that gentlemen have their peculiar ways?'

'I did, sir. I trust the observation was not impertinent.'

'According to Mr Robert, Mr Darien-Gore himself happened to recount at the dinner table some legend or superstition about the well. It was to the effect that notable good luck will be won by any man who makes his way to the well at midnight, stands on its wall and invocates the moon.'

'Does *what*?' General Strickland exclaimed. 'Some pagan nonsense, eh? God bless my soul!'

'It's perfectly true.' Jasper spoke slowly. 'I did spin that old yarn. And I can imagine some young man – a subaltern, or undergraduate, for instance – who might have received it as a dare. But not that fellow Jolly. He wasn't the type. It doesn't make sense.'

'Unfortunately, something further happened.' Appleby still stood in front of the fireplace; he might almost have been on guard before it. 'Mr Robert – so he tells me – made some sort of wager with Jolly. Or perhaps he did no more than vaguely suggest a wager. He was trying, as I understand the matter, to entertain the man – who was not altogether in his element among us. Have I got it right?'

Most of the company were standing or sitting in a wide circle round Appleby. But Robert had sat down a little apart. He might have been taking up, quite consciously, an isolated and alienated pose – rather suggestive of young Hamlet at the court of his uncle, Claudius. He had remained silent so far. But now he replied to Appleby's challenge.

'Yes,' he said. 'Just that. I said something about a bottle of Jasper's Margaux if Jolly could tell me in the morning that he had done this stupid and foolhardy thing. I repent it bitterly. In fact, I hold myself responsible for the man's death.'

'Come, come,' General Strickland said kindly. 'That's a morbid view, my dear Robert. You were doing your best to entertain the fellow, and what has happened couldn't be foreseen.'

'It isn't the truth! It can't be!' Prunella had sprung to her feet in some ungovernable agitation. 'He still wasn't that sort of man. He was calculating … cold. I hated him.' She turned to her husband. 'Robert – you're not hiding something … shielding somebody?'

'Prunella, for God's sake control yourself.' Robert made what was almost a weary gesture. 'It's a queer story, I know. But there it is.'

'Which puts the matter in a nutshell.' Appleby had taken

a single step forward, and the effect was to make him oddly dominate the people in the long gallery. 'It's a queer story. But it's conceivable. And there isn't any other in the field. Not unless we have a few more facts. As it happens, we *have* more facts. The first of them is a bow-shot in the night. Strickland, would you mind stepping through that door at the end of the gallery, and bringing in anything you find hidden behind it?'

General Strickland did as he was asked, and came back carrying a bow.

'It's a bow,' he said – a shade obviously. 'And there's an arrow there too.'

'Precisely. And somebody was concerned to return them to the ascham here within the last hour. Frape appears to be convinced that that person was Mr Trevor. So perhaps Mr Trevor somehow lured Jolly up on the lip of the well, and then – so to speak – shot him into it. One moment!' Appleby stopped Trevor on the verge of some outburst. 'Another fact is this: Jolly was, to my knowledge, a professional blackmailer. And his arrival here wasn't fortuitous; it was designed. Moreover – but this is conjecture rather than fact – he and Mr Trevor were not entirely unknown to each other – '

'*That's* true.' Charles Trevor was a frightened man. 'I had an … an encounter with Jolly in the past. Suddenly coming upon him again was a great shock. But it wasn't – '

'Very well. Suppose Frape didn't see Mr Trevor peering through that door. Supposing he was concerned to shield – '

'Of course Frape saw *me*. And then *you* discovered me. And now Strickland has discovered the bow and arrow.'

Robert Darien-Gore got these statements out in a series of gasps. 'I haven't been sleeping. Last night I knew it wasn't even worthwhile going to bed. So I passed the time repairing one of the horns of that bow, and feathering an arrow. Then I brought them back here.' Looking round the company, Robert met absolute silence. 'I give you all my word of honour as a gentleman,' he said, 'that I did not shoot Jolly.'

There was another long silence, broken only by an inarticulate sound from Prunella.

'We can accept that,' Appleby said gently. 'But you killed him, all the same.'

'Jolly came to Gore Castle in the way of trade,' Appleby said. 'His own filthy trade. He had papers he was going to sell – at a price. I don't know what story these papers tell. But it is the story that failed to see the light of day when Robert Darien-Gore had to leave the army. Jolly, I may say, made a sinister joke to me. He said he knew when he'd been given enough; he knew just how much he could take. He was wrong.'

'This must stop.' Jasper Darien-Gore spoke with an assumption of authority. 'If there is matter for the police to investigate, then the local police must be summoned in a regular way. Sir John, I consider that you have no standing in this matter. And it is an abuse – '

'You are quite wrong, sir.' Appleby looked sternly at his host. 'I am the holder of a warrant card, like any other officer of the police. And on its authority I propose to make an arrest on a specific charge. Now, may I go on?'

'For God's sake do!' Prunella cried out. 'I can't stand more of this … I can't stand it!'

'My dear,' Mrs Strickland said, and went to sit beside her.

'Strickland – take the binoculars again, will you? Look at the keep. Got it? What strikes you about it?'

'Chiefly the scaffolding round it, I'd say.'

'Windows?'

'There are narrow windows all the way up – lighting a spiral staircase, I seem to remember?'

'Glazed?'

'No?'

'Imagine a skilled archer near ground-level on the near side of the bailey. Could he get an arrow through one of those windows?'

'I suppose he could. First shot, if he was first class.'

'And on a flight that would pass over the well?'

'Certainly.'

'That was what happened. That was the bow-shot I heard and Frape heard. The arrow carried a line – by means of which somebody in the keep could draw a strong nylon cord across the bailey, something more than head-high above the well.' Appleby turned to Robert. 'You had already killed Jolly – simply with an arrow employed as a dagger, I rather think. He was a meagre little man. You carried the body to the well, pitched it in, mounted the lip – and returned across the bailey on the cord. For a climber, it wasn't a particularly difficult feat. Then the line was released at the other end, swung like a skipping rope until it fell near one of the flanking walls and drawn gently back through the snow. There will be virtually no trace of it. It only remained to return the bow to the ascham here. The bow and one arrow. The second missing arrow is … with Jolly, I rather think.'

'You know too much.' Robert Darien-Gore had been sitting hunched in a chair, his right hand deep in the pocket of his shooting jacket. Now he sprang to his feet, brought out his hand and hurled something in the direction of Appleby, which flew past him and into the fireplace. Then the hand went back again, and came out holding something else. The crack of a pistol reverberated in the gallery as Robert crashed to the floor.

'*By God – he's dead!*' Like a flash, Jasper had been on his knees beside his brother. But now he rose, dazed and staggering – and with the pistol in his hands. He came slowly over to Appleby. 'I think,' he said, 'my brother is ... dead. Will you ... see?'

Appleby took a couple of steps forward – and as he did so, Jasper dived behind him. What Robert had hurled into the fireplace was Jolly's pocketbook; it had missed the fire, and lay undamaged. Jasper grabbed it just as Appleby turned, and made to thrust it into the heart of the flame. Appleby knocked up his arm, and the pocketbook went flying across the gallery. Jasper eluded Appleby's grasp, vaulted a settee with the effortlessness of a young athlete in training, retrieved the pocketbook and turned round to face the company. He still had Robert's pistol in his hand.

'Don't move,' he said. 'Don't any of you move.'

'This is foolish,' Appleby said quietly. 'Foolish and useless. Your brother is indeed dead. And his last day's work has been to involve you in murder. You knew nothing about Jolly when he arrived – except that you distrusted him. But Robert made you receive him as a guest, and by dinner time Robert had persuaded you to his plot. Your own first part in it was to concoct that legend about the well. But your main part was to be in the keep when the arrow arrived. You face a charge of murder, just as your brother would have done. Nothing is to be gained by waving a pistol.'

'All of you get back from that fire – now.' With raised pistol, Jasper took a pace towards Appleby. In his other hand he raised the pocketbook. 'What I hold here, I burn. After that, we can talk.'

'I'm sorry, Darien-Gore, but it won't do. Before you burn those papers, you'll have shot a policeman in the course of his duty. And if – '

'Permit me, sir.' Frape had stepped forward. He walked past Appleby and advanced upon his employer. 'It will be best, sir, that you should give me the gun.'

'Stand back, Frape, or I shoot.'

'As Sir John says, sir, it won't do. So, with great respect, I must insist.' And Frape put out a steady arm and took the pistol from his employer's hand. 'Thank you, sir. I am obliged to you.'

For a fraction of a second Jasper looked merely bewildered. Then, as Appleby again advanced upon him, he turned and ran from the gallery.

'Frape – help me to get him.' Instinctively, Appleby addressed first the man who had proved himself. He was already running down the gallery as he called over his shoulder. 'Strickland, Trevor – he must be stopped.'

VIII

The chase through Gore Castle took place in the first light of a bleak winter dawn. Judith Appleby, who had followed the men, was to remember it as a confusion of panting and shouting, with ill-identified figures vanishing down vistas that were composed sometimes of stately rooms in unending sequence, sometimes of narrow defiles through forbidding medieval masonry. It was the kind of pursuit that may happen in a nightmare: in one instant hopelessly at fault, and in the next an all but triumphant breathing down the hunted man's neck.

They were in the open – plunging and kicking through snow. Suddenly, in front of Jasper as he rounded a corner, there seemed to be only a high blank wall. But he ran straight at it; a buttress appeared; in the angle of this stood a ladder, steeply pitched. Appleby and Frape were at its foot seconds after Jasper's heels had vanished up it; but even as they were about to mount it, it came down past their heads. As they struggled to set it up again Judith could see that Jasper, with a brief respite won, was crouched down on a narrow ledge, and fumbling in a pocket. With trembling hands he produced a box of matches – and then Jolly's fatal pocketbook. From this he pulled out a first sheet of paper, crumpled it, struck a match. But the match – and then a second and a third – went out. And now the ladder was in place again. There was no time for another attempt. Clutching the pocketbook, Jasper rose and ran on. He vanished through a low archway. He had gained the keep.

It was almost dark inside. Judith was now abreast of her husband. As they paused to accustom themselves to the gloom, Jasper's voice came from somewhere above.

'Are you there, Appleby? I don't advise the climb.'

'Darien-Gore, come down – in the name of the law.'

'This is my keep, Appleby. It was to defy the law – didn't I tell you? – that my ancestors built it long ago.'

The last words were almost inaudible, for Jasper was climbing again. They followed. Perpendicular slits of light spiralled downwards and past them as they panted up the winding stair. Quite suddenly, there was open sky in front of them, and against it Jasper's figure in silhouette. In front of him was a criss-cross of scaffolding. One aspect of it they had seen from other angles already: a wooden plank, thrusting out into vacancy for some feet – and startlingly suggestive of a springboard. Beyond it, the eye could only travel vertiginously down ... to the inner bailey, the well, the single set of prints across the snow.

Jasper turned for a moment. They could see his features dimly, and then – very clearly – that he was holding up the pocketbook to them in a gesture of defiance. He thrust it into a pocket, turned away, measured his distance and ran. It was not a jump; it was the sort of dive that earns a high score in an Olympic pool. In a beautiful curve, Jasper Darien-Gore rose, pivoted in the air, plunged, diminished in free fall and vanished (as they ceased to be able to bear to look) into the well.

And from behind them came the breathless voice of General Strickland: 'Good God, Appleby! Jasper didn't better that one when he gained a Gold for England in '36.'

A Scandal in Winter

Gillian Linscott

At first Silver Stick and his Square Bear were no more to us than incidental diversions at the Hotel Edelweiss. The Edelweiss at Christmas and the new year was like a sparkling white desert island, or a very luxurious ocean liner sailing throughout snow instead of sea. There we were, a hundred people or so, cut off from the rest of the world, even from the rest of Switzerland, with only each other for entertainment or company. It was one of the only possible hotels to stay at in 1910 for this new fad of winter sporting. The smaller Berghaus across the way was not one of the possible hotels, so its dozen or so visitors hardly counted. As for the villagers in their wooden chalets with the cows living downstairs, they didn't count at all. Occasionally on walks Amanda and I would see them carrying in logs from neatly stacked wood-piles or carrying out forkfuls of warm soiled straw that sent columns of white steam into the blue air. They were part of the valley, like the rocks and pine trees, but they didn't ski or skate, so they had no place in our world – apart from the sleighs. There were two of those in the village. One, a sober affair drawn by a stolid bay cob with a few token bells on the harness, brought guests and their luggage from the nearest railway station. The other, the one that mattered to Amanda and me, was a streak of black and scarlet, swift as the mountain wind, clamorous with silver bells, drawn by a sleek little honey-coloured Haflinger with a silvery mane and tail that matched the bells. A pleasure sleigh, with no purpose in life beyond amusing the guests at the Edelweiss. We'd see it drawn up in the trampled snow outside, the handsome young owner with his long whip and blond moustache waiting patiently. Sometimes we'd be allowed to linger and watch as he helped in a lady and gentleman and adjusted the white fur rug over their laps. Then away they'd go, hissing and jingling through the snow, into the track through the pine forest. Amanda and I had been promised that, as a treat on New Year's Day, we would be taken for a ride in it. We looked forward to it more eagerly than Christmas.

But that was ten days away and until then we had to amuse ourselves. We skated on the rink behind the hotel. We waved goodbye to our father when he went off in the mornings with his skis and his guide. We sat on the hotel terrace drinking hot chocolate with blobs of cream on top while Mother wrote and read letters. When we thought Mother wasn't watching, Amanda and I would compete to see if we could drink all the chocolate so that the blob of cream stayed marooned at the bottom of the cup, to be eaten in luscious and impolite spoonfuls. If she glanced up and caught us, Mother would tell us not to be so childish, which, since Amanda was eleven and I was nearly thirteen, was fair enough, but we had to get what entertainment we could out of the chocolate. The truth was that we were all of us, most of the time, bored out of our wits. Which was why we turned our attention to the affairs of the other guests and Amanda and I had our ears permanently tuned to the small dramas of the adults' conversation.

'I still can't believe she will.'

'Well, that's what the head waiter said, and he should know. She's reserved the table in the corner overlooking the terrace and said they should be sure to have the Tokay.'

'The same table as last year.'

'The same wine, too.'

Our parents looked at each other over the croissants, carefully not noticing the maid as she poured our coffee. ('One doesn't notice the servants, dear, it only makes them awkward.')

'I'm sure it's not true. Any woman with any feeling ...'

'What makes you think she has any?'

Silence, as eye signals went on over our heads. I knew what was being signalled, just as I'd known what was being discussed in an overheard scrap of conversation between our parents at bedtime the night we arrived: ' ... effect it might have on Jessica.' My name. I came rapidly out of drowsiness, kept my eyes closed but listened.

'I don't think we need worry about that. Jessica's tougher than you think.' My mother's voice. She needed us to be tough so that she didn't have to waste time worrying about us.

'All the same, she must remember it. It is only a year ago. That sort of experience can mark a child for life.'

'Darling, they don't react like we do. They're much more callous at that age.'

Even with eyes closed I could tell from the quality of my father's silence that he wasn't convinced, but it was no use arguing with Mother's certainties. They switched the light off and closed the door. For a minute or two I lay awake in the dark wondering whether I was marked for life by what I'd seen and how it would show, then I wondered instead whether I'd ever be able to do pirouettes on the ice like the girl from Paris, and fell asleep in a wistful dream of bells and the hiss of skates.

The conversation between our parents that breakfast time over what she would or wouldn't do was interrupted by the little stir of two other guests being shown to their table. Amanda caught my eye.

'Silver Stick and his Square Bear are going skiing.'

Both gentlemen – elderly gentlemen as it seemed to us, but they were probably no older than their late fifties – were wearing heavy wool jumpers, tweed breeches and thick socks, just as father was. He nodded to them across the tables, wished them good morning and received nods and good-mornings back. Even the heavy sports clothing couldn't take away the oddity and distinction from the tall man. He was, I think, the thinnest person I'd ever seen. He didn't stoop as so many tall older people did but walked upright and lightly. His face, with its eagle's beak of a nose, was deeply tanned, like some of the older inhabitants of the village, but unlike them it was without wrinkles apart from two deep folds from the nose to the corners of his mouth. His hair was what had struck us most. It clung smoothly to his head in a cap of pure and polished silver, like the knob on an expensive walking stick. His companion, large and square-shouldered in any case, looked more so in his skiing clothes. He shambled and tended to trip over chairs. He had a round, amiable face with pale, rather watery eyes, a clipped grey moustache but no more than a fringe of hair left on his gleaming pate. He always smiled at us when we met on the terrace or in corridors and appeared kindly. We'd noticed that he was always doing things for Silver Stick, pouring his coffee, posting his letters. For this reason we'd got it into our heads that Square Bear was Silver Stick's keeper. Amanda said Silver Stick probably went mad at the full moon and Square Bear had to lock him up and sing loudly so that people wouldn't hear his howling. She kept asking people when the next full moon would be, but so far nobody knew. I thought he'd probably come to Switzerland because he was dying of consumption, which explained the thinness, and Square Bear was his doctor. I listened for a coughing fit to confirm this, but so far there'd been not a sign of one. As they settled to their breakfast we watched as much as we could without being rebuked for staring. Square Bear opened the paper that had been lying beside his plate and read things out to Silver Stick, who gave the occasional little nod over his coffee, as if he'd known whatever it was all the time. It was the *Times* of London and must have been at least two days old because it had to come up from the station in the sleigh.

Amanda whispered: 'He eats.'

The waiter had brought a rack of toast and a stone jar of Oxford marmalade to their table instead of croissants. Stick was eating toast like any normal person. Father asked: 'Who eats?'

We indicated with our eyes.

'Well, why shouldn't he eat? You need a lot of energy for skiing.'

Mother, taking an interest for once, said they seemed old for skiing.

'You'd be surprised. Dr Watson's not bad, but as for the other one – well, he went past me like a bird in places so steep that even the guide didn't want to try it. And stayed standing up at the end of it when most of us would have been just a big hole in the snow. The man's so rational he's completely without fear. It's fear that wrecks you when you're skiing. You come to a steep place, you think you're going to fall and nine times out of ten you do fall. Holmes comes to the same steep place, doesn't see any reason why he can't do it – so he does it.' My mother said that anybody really rational would have the sense not to go skiing in the first place. My ear had been caught by one word.

'Square Bear's a doctor? Is Silver Stick ill?'

'Not that I know. Is there any more coffee in that pot?'

And there we left it for the while. You might say that Amanda and I should have known at once who they were, and I suppose nine out of ten children in Europe would have known. But we'd led an unusual life, mainly on account of Mother, and although we knew many things unknown to most girls of our age, we were ignorant of a lot of others that were common currency.

We waved off Father and his guide as they went wallowing up in the deep snow through the pine trees, skis on their shoulders, then turned back for our skates. We stopped at the driveway to let the sober black sleigh go past, the one that went down the valley to the railway. There was nobody in the back, but the rugs were ready and neatly folded.

'Somebody new coming,' Amanda said.

I knew Mother was looking at me, but she said nothing. Amanda and I were indoors doing our holiday reading when the sleigh came back, so we didn't see who was in it, but when we went downstairs later there was a humming tension about the hotel, like the feeling you get when a violinist is holding his bow just above the string and the tingle of the note runs up and down your spine before you hear it. It was only mid-afternoon but dusk was already settling on the valley. We were allowed a last walk outside before it got dark, and made as usual for the skating rink. Coloured electric lights were throwing patches of yellow, red and blue on the dark surface. The lame man with the accordion was playing a Strauss waltz and a few couples were skating to it, though not very well. More were clustered round the charcoal brazier at the edge of the rink, where a waiter poured small glasses of mulled wine. Perhaps the man with the accordion knew the dancers were getting tired or wanted to go home himself, because when the waltz ended he changed to something wild and gypsy-sounding, harder to dance to. The couples on the ice tried it for a few steps then gave up, laughing, to join the others round the brazier. For a while the ice was empty and the lame man played on to the dusk and the dark mountains.

Then a figure came gliding onto the ice. There was a decisiveness about the way she did it that marked her out at once from the other skaters. They'd come on staggering or swaggering, depending on whether they were beginners or thought themselves expert, but staggerers and swaggerers alike had a self-conscious air, knowing that this was not their natural habitat. She took to the ice like a swan to the water or a swallow to the air. The laughter died away, the drinking stopped and we watched as she swooped and dipped and circled all alone to the gypsy music. There were no showy pirouettes like the girl from Paris, no folding of the arms and look-at-me smiles. It's quite likely that she was not a particularly expert skater, that what was so remarkable about it was her willingness to take the rink, the music, the attention as hers by right. She wasn't even dressed for skating. The black skirt coming to within a few inches of the instep of her skate boots, the black mink jacket, the matching cap, were probably what she'd been wearing on the journey up from the station. But she'd been ready for this, had planned to announce her return exactly this way.

Her return. At first, absorbed by the performance, I hadn't recognised her. I'd registered that she was not a young woman and that she was elegant. It was when a little of my attention came back to my mother that I knew. She was standing there as stiff and prickly as one of the pine trees, staring at the figure on the ice like everybody else, but it wasn't admiration on her face, more a kind of horror. They were all looking like that, all the adults, as if she were the messenger of something dangerous. Then a woman's voice, not my mother's, said, 'How could she? Really, how could she?'

There was a murmuring of agreement and I could feel the horror changing to something more commonplace – social disapproval. Once the first words had been said, others followed and there was a rustling of sharp little phrases like a sledge runner grating on gravel.

'Only a year ... to come here again ... no respect ... lucky not to be ... after what happened.'

My mother put a firm hand on each of our shoulders. 'Time for your tea.'

Normally we'd have protested, begged for another few minutes, but we knew that this was serious. To get into the hotel from the ice rink you go up some steps from the back terrace and in at the big glass doors to the breakfast room. There were two men standing on the terrace. From there you could see the rink, and they were staring down at what was happening. Silver Stick and Square Bear. I saw the thin man's eyes in the light from the breakfast room. They were harder and more intent than anything I'd ever seen, harder than the ice itself. Normally, being properly brought up, we'd have said good evening to them as we went, but Mother propelled us inside without speaking. As soon as she'd got us settled at the table she went to find Father, who'd be back from skiing by then. I knew they'd be talking about me and felt important, but concerned that I couldn't live up to that importance. After all, what I'd seen had lasted only a few seconds and I hadn't felt any of the things I was supposed to feel. I'd never known him before it happened, apart from seeing him across the dining room a few times, and I hadn't even known he was dead until they told me afterwards.

What happened at dinner that evening was like the ice rink, only without gypsy music. That holiday Amanda and I were allowed to come down to dinner with our parents for the soup course. After the soup we were supposed to say good night politely and go up and put ourselves to bed. People who'd been skating and skiing all day were hungry by evening, so usually attention was concentrated discreetly on the swing doors to the kitchen and the procession of waiters with the silver tureens. That night was different. The focus of attention was one small table in the corner of the room beside the window. A table laid like the rest of them with white linen, silver cutlery, gold-bordered plates and a little array of crystal glasses. A table for one. An empty table.

My father said: 'Looks as if she's funked it. Can't say I blame her.'

My mother gave him one of her 'be quiet' looks, announced that this was our evening for speaking French and asked me in that language to pass her some bread, if I pleased.

I had my back to the door and my hand on the bread basket. All I knew was that the room went quiet.

'Don't turn round,' my mother hissed in English. I turned round and there she was, in black velvet and diamonds. Her hair, with more streaks of grey than I remembered from the year before, was swept up and secured with a pearl-and-diamond comb. The previous year, before the thing happened, my mother had remarked that she was surprisingly slim for a retired opera singer. This year she was thin, cheek bones and collarbones above the black velvet bodice sharp enough to cut paper. She was inclining her elegant head towards the headwaiter, probably listening to words of welcome. He was smiling, but then he smiled at everybody. Nobody else smiled as she followed him to the table in the far, the very far, corner. You could hear the creak of necks screwing themselves away from her. No entrance she ever made in her stage career could have been as nerve-racking as that long walk across the hotel floor. In spite of the silent commands now radiating from my mother, I could no more have turned away from her than from Blondin crossing Niagara Falls. My disobedience was rewarded, as disobedience so often is, because I saw it happen. In the middle of that silent dining room, amid a hundred or so people pretending not to notice her, I saw Silver Stick get to his feet. Among all those seated people he looked even taller than before, his burnished silver head gleaming like snow on the Matterhorn above that rock ridge of a nose, below it the glacial white and black of his evening clothes. Square Bear hesitated for a moment, then followed his example. As in her lonely walk she came alongside their table, Silver Stick bowed with the dignity of a man who did not have to bow very often, and again Square Bear copied him, less elegantly. Square Bear's face was red and flustered, but the other man's hadn't altered. She paused for a moment, gravely returned their bows with a bend of her white neck then walked on. The silence through the room lasted until the head waiter pulled out her chair and she sat down at her table, then, as if on cue, the waiters with their tureens came marching through the swinging doors, and the babble and the clash of cutlery sounded as loud as war starting.

At breakfast I asked Mother: 'Why did they bow to her?' I knew it was a banned subject, but I knew too that I was in an obscurely privileged position, because of the effect all this was supposed to be having on me. I wondered when it would come out, like secret writing on a laurel leaf you keep close to your chest to warm it. When I was fourteen, eighteen?

'Don't ask silly questions. And you don't need two lumps of sugar in your café au lait.'

Father suggested a trip to the town down the valley after lunch, to buy Christmas presents. It was meant as a distraction and it worked to an extent, but I still couldn't get her out of my mind. Later that morning, when I was supposed to be having a healthy snowball fight with boring children, I wandered away to the back terrace overlooking the ice rink. I hoped that I might find her there again, but it was occupied by noisy beginners, slithering and screeching. I despised them for their ordinariness.

I'd turned away and was looking at the back of the hotel, thinking no particular thoughts, when I heard footsteps behind me and a voice said: 'Was that where you were standing when it happened?'

It was the first time I'd heard Silver Stick's voice at close quarters. It was a pleasant voice, deep but clear, like the sea in a cave. He was standing there in his rough tweed jacket and cap with earflaps only a few yards away from me. Square Bear stood behind him, looking anxious, neck muffled in a woollen scarf. I considered, looked up at the roof again and down to my feet.

'Yes, it must have been about here.'

'Holmes, don't you think we should ask this little girl's mother? She might ...'

'My mother wasn't there. I was.'

Perhaps I'd learned something already about taking the centre of the stage. The thought came to me that it would be a great thing if he bowed to me, as he'd bowed to her.

'Quite so.'

He didn't bow, but he seemed pleased.

'You see, Watson, Miss Jessica isn't in the least hysterical about it, are you?'

I saw that he meant that as a compliment, so I gave him the little inclination of the head that I'd been practising in front of the mirror when Amanda wasn't looking. He smiled, and there was more warmth in the smile than seemed likely from the height and sharpness of him.

'I take it that you have no objection to talking about what you saw.'

I said graciously: 'Not in the very least.' Then honesty compelled me to spoil it by adding, 'Only I didn't see very much.'

'It's not how much you saw, but how clearly you saw it. I wonder if you'd kindly tell Dr Watson and me exactly what you saw, in as much detail as you can remember.'

The voice was gentle, but there was no gentleness in the dark eyes fixed on me. I don't mean they were hard or cruel, simply that emotion of any sort had no more part in them than in the lens of a camera or telescope. They gave me an odd feeling, not fear exactly, but as if I'd become real in a way I hadn't quite been before. I knew that being clear about what I'd seen that day a year ago mattered more than anything I'd ever done. I closed my eyes and thought hard.

'I was standing just here. I was waiting for Mother and

Amanda because we were going out for a walk and Amanda had lost one of her fur gloves as usual. I saw him falling, then he hit the roof over the dining room and came sliding down it. The snow started moving as well, so he came down with the snow. He landed just over there, where that chair is, and all the rest of the snow came down on top of him, so you could only see his arm sticking out. The arm wasn't moving, but I didn't know he was dead. A lot of people came running and started pushing the snow away from him, then somebody said I shouldn't be there so they took me away to find Mother, so I wasn't there when they got the snow off him.'

I stopped, short of breath. Square Bear was looking ill at ease and pitying, but Silver Stick's eyes hadn't changed.

'When you were waiting for your mother and sister, which way were you facing?'

'The rink. I was watching the skaters.'

'Quite so. That meant you were facing away from the hotel.'

'Yes.'

'And yet you saw the man falling?'

'Yes.'

'What made you turn round?'

I'd no doubt about that. It was the part of my story that everybody had been most concerned with at the time.

'He shouted.'

'Shouted what?'

'Shouted "No".'

'When did he shout it?'

I hesitated. Nobody had asked me that before because the answer was obvious.

'When he fell.'

'Of course, but at what point during his fall? I take it that it was before he landed on the roof over the dining room or you wouldn't have turned round in time to see it.'

'Yes.'

'And you turned round in time to see him in the air and falling?'

'Holmes, I don't think you should …'

'Oh, do be quiet, Watson. Well, Miss Jessica?'

'Yes, he was in the air and falling.'

'And he'd already screamed by then. So at what point did he scream?'

I wanted to be clever and grown-up, to make him think well of me.

'I suppose it was when she pushed him out of the window.'

It was Square Bear's face that showed most emotion. He screwed up his eyes, went red and made little imploring signs with his fur-mittened hands, causing him to look more bear-like than ever. This time the protest was not at his friend, but at me. Silver Stick put up a hand to stop him saying anything, but his face had changed too, with a sharp V on the forehead. The voice was a shade less gentle.

'When who pushed him out of the window?'

'His wife, Mrs McEvoy.'

I wondered whether to add, 'The woman you bowed to last night,' but decided against it.

'Did you see her push him?'

'No.'

'Did you see Mrs McEvoy at the window?'

'No.'

'And yet you tell me that Mrs McEvoy pushed her husband out of the window. Why?'

'Everybody knows she did.'

I knew from the expression on Square Bear's face that I'd gone badly wrong, but couldn't see where. He, kindly man, must have guessed that because he started trying to explain to me.

'You see, my dear, after many years with my good friend Mr Holmes ...'

Yet again he was waved into silence.

'Miss Jessica, Dr Watson means well but I hope he will permit me to speak for myself. It's a fallacy to believe that age in itself brings wisdom, but one thing it infallibly brings is experience. Will you permit me, from my experience if not from my wisdom, to offer you a little advice?'

I nodded, not gracious now, just awed.

'Then my advice is this: always remember that what everybody knows, nobody knows.'

He used that voice like a skater uses his weight on the blade to skim or turn.

'You say everybody knows that Mrs McEvoy pushed her husband out of the window. As far as I know, you are the only person in the world who saw Mr McEvoy fall. And yet, as you've told me, you did not see Mrs McEvoy push him. So who is this "everybody" who can claim such certainty about an event which, as far as we know, nobody witnessed?'

It's miserable not knowing answers. What is nineteen times three? What is the past participle of the verb *faire?* I wanted to live up to him, but unwittingly he'd pressed the button that brought on the panic of the schoolroom. I blurted out: 'He was very rich and she didn't love him, and now she's very rich and can do what she likes.'

Again the bear's fur mitts went up, scrabbling the air. Again he was disregarded.

'So Mrs McEvoy is rich and can do what she likes? Does it strike you that she's happy?'

'Holmes, how can a child know …?'

I thought of the gypsy music, the gleaming dark fur, the pearls in her hair. I found myself shaking my head.

'No. And yet she comes here again, exactly a year after her husband died, the very place in the world that you'd expect her to avoid at all costs. She comes here knowing what people are saying about her, making sure everybody has a chance to see her, holding her head high. Have you any idea what that must do to a woman?'

This time Square Bear really did protest and went on protesting. How could he expect a child to know about the feelings of a mature woman? How could I be blamed for repeating the gossip of my elders? Really, Holmes, it was too much. This time too Silver Stick seemed to agree with him. He smoothed out the V shape in his forehead and apologised.

'Let us, if we may, return to the surer ground of what you actually saw. I take it that the hotel has not been rebuilt in any way since last year.'

I turned again to look at the back of the hotel. As far as I could see, it was just as it had been, the glass doors leading from the dining room and breakfast room onto the terrace, a tiled sloping roof above them. Then, joined onto the roof, the three main guest floors of the hotel. The top two floors were the ones that most people took because they had wrought-iron balconies where, on sunny days, you could stand to look at the mountains. Below them were the smaller rooms. They were less popular because, being directly above the kitchen and dining room, they suffer from noise and cooking smells and had no balconies.

Silver Stick said to Square Bear, 'That was the room they had last year, top floor, second from the right. So if he were pushed, he'd have to be pushed over the balcony as well as out of the window. That would take quite a lot of strength, wouldn't you say?'

The next question was to me. He asked if I'd seen Mr McEvoy before he fell out of the window and I said yes, a few times.

'Was he a small man?'

'No, quite big.'

'The same size as Dr Watson here, for instance?'

Square Bear straightened his broad shoulders, as if for military inspection.

'He was fatter.'

'Younger or older?'

'Quite old. As old as you are.'

Square Bear made a chuffing sound, and his shoulders slumped a little.

'So we have a man about the same age as our friend Watson and heavier. Difficult, wouldn't you say, for any woman to push him anywhere against his will?'

'Perhaps she took him by surprise, told him to lean out and look at something, then swept his legs off the floor.'

That wasn't my own theory. The event had naturally been

analysed in all its aspects the year before, and all the parental care in the world couldn't have kept it from me.

'A touching picture. Shall we come back to things we know for certain? What about the snow? Was there as much snow as this last year?'

'I think so. It came up above my knees last year. It doesn't quite this year, but then I've grown.'

Square Bear murmured: 'They'll keep records of that sort of thing.'

'Just so, but we're also grateful for Miss Jessica's calibrations. May we trouble you with just one more question?'

I said yes rather warily.

'You've told us that just before you turned round and saw him falling you heard him shout "No". What sort of "No" was it?'

I was puzzled. Nobody had asked me that before.

'Was it an angry "No?" A protesting "No"? The kind of "No" you'd shout if somebody were pushing you over a balcony?'

The other man looked as if he wanted to protest again but kept quiet. The intensity in Silver Stick's eyes would have frozen a brook in mid-babble. When I didn't answer at once he visibly made himself relax and his voice went softer.

'It's hard for you to remember, isn't it? Everybody was so sure that it was one particular sort of "No" that they've fixed their version in your mind. I want you to do something for me, if you would be so kind. I want you to forget that Dr Watson and I are here and stand and look down at the ice rink just as you were doing last year. I want you to clear your mind of everything else and think that it really is last year and you're hearing that shout for the first time. Will you do that?'

I faced away from them. First I looked at this year's skaters, then I closed my eyes and tried to remember how it had been. I felt the green itchy scarf round my neck, the cold getting to my toes and fingers as I waited. I heard the cry and it was all I could do not to turn round and see the body tumbling again. When I opened my eyes and looked at them they were still waiting patiently.

'I think I've remembered.'

'And what sort of "No" was it?'

It was clear in my mind but hard to put into words.

'It … it was as if he'd been going to say something else if he'd had time. Not just no. No something.'

'No something what?'

More silence while I thought about it, then a prompt from Square Bear.

'Could it have been a name, my dear?'

'Don't put any more ideas into her head. You thought he was going to say something after the no, but you don't know what, is that it?'

'Yes, like no running, or no cakes today, only that wasn't it. Something you couldn't do.'

'Or something not there, like the cakes?'

'Yes, something like that. Only it couldn't have been, could it?'

'Couldn't? If something happened in a particular way, then it happened, and there's no could or couldn't about it.'

It was the kind of thing governesses said, but he was smiling now and I had the idea that something I'd said had pleased him. 'I see your mother and sister coming, so I'm afraid we must end this very useful conversation. I am much obliged to you for your powers of observation. Will you permit me to ask you some more questions if any more occur to me?'

I nodded.

'Is it a secret?'

'Do you want it to be?'

'Holmes, I don't think you should encourage this young lady …'

'My dear Watson, in my observation there's nothing more precious you can give a child to keep than a secret.'

My mother came across the terrace with Amanda. Silver Stick and Square Bear touched their hats to her and hoped we enjoyed our walk. When she asked me later what we'd been talking about, I said they'd asked whether the snow was as deep last year and hugged the secret of my partnership. I became in my imagination eyes and ears for him. At the children's party at teatime on Christmas Eve the parents talked in low tones, believing that we were absorbed in the present-giving round the hotel tree. But it would have taken more than the porter in red robe and white whiskers or his largesse of three wooden geese on a string to distract me from my work. I listened and stored up every scrap against the time when he'd ask me questions again. And I watched Mrs McEvoy as she went round the hotel through Christmas Eve and Christmas Day, pale and upright in her black and her jewels, trailing silence after her like the long train of a dress.

My call came on Boxing Day. There was another snowball fight in the hotel grounds, for parents as well this time.

I stood back from it all and waited by a little clump of bare birches and, sure enough, Silver Stick and Square Bear came walking over to me.

'I've found out a lot about her,' I said.

'Have you indeed?'

'He was her second husband. She had another one she loved more, but he died of a fever. It was when they were visiting Egypt a long time ago.'

'Ten years ago.'

Silver Stick's voice was remote. He wasn't even looking at me.

'She got married to Mr McEvoy three years ago. Most people said it was for his money, but there was an American lady at the party and she said Mr McEvoy seemed quite nice when you first knew him and he was interested in music and singers, so perhaps it was one of those marriages where people quite like each other without being in love, you know?'

I thought I'd managed that rather well. I'd tried to make it like my mother talking to her friends, and it sounded convincing in my ears. I was disappointed at the lack of reaction, so brought up my big guns.

'Only she didn't stay liking him because after they got married she found out about his eye.'

'His eye?'

A reaction at last, but from Square Bear, not Silver Stick. I grabbed for the right word and clung to it.

'Roving. It was a roving eye. He kept looking at other ladies, and she didn't like it.'

I hoped they'd understand that it meant looking in a

special way. I didn't know myself exactly what special way, but the adults talking among themselves at the party had certainly understood. But it seemed I'd overestimated these two because they were just standing there staring at me. Perhaps Silver Stick wasn't as clever as I'd thought. I threw in my last little oddment of information, something anybody could understand.

'I found out her first name. It's Irene.'

Square Bear cleared his throat. Silver Stick said nothing. He was looking over my head at the snowball fight.

'Holmes, I really think we should leave Jessica to play with her little friends.'

'Not yet. There's something I wanted to ask her. Do you remember the staff at the hotel last Christmas?'

Here was a dreadful comedown. I'd brought him a head richly crammed with love, money and marriages, and he was asking about the domestics. Perhaps the disappointment on my face looked like stupidity because his voice became impatient.

'The people who looked after you, the porters and the waiters and the maids, especially the maids.'

'They're the same … I think.' I was running them through my head. There was Petra with her thick plaits who brought us our cups of chocolate, fat Renata who made our beds, grey-haired Ulrike with her limp.

'None left?'

'I don't think so.'

Then the memory came to me of blond curls escaping from a maid's uniform cap and a clear voice singing as she swept the corridors, blithe as a bird.

'There was Eva, but she got married.'

'Who did she marry?'

'Franz, the man who's got the sleigh.'

It was flying down the drive as I spoke, silver bells jangling, the little horse gold in the sunshine. 'A good marriage for a hotel maid.'

'Oh, he didn't have the sleigh last year. He was only the under-porter.'

'Indeed. Watson, I think we must have a ride in this sleigh. Will you see the head porter about booking it?'

I hoped he might invite me to go with them but he said nothing about that. Still, he seemed to be in a good temper again – although I couldn't see that it was from anything I'd told him.

'Miss Jessica, again I'm obliged to you. I may have yet another favour to ask, but all in good time.'

I went reluctantly to join the snowballers as the two of them walked through the snow back to the hotel.

That afternoon, on our walk, they went past us on their way down the drive in Franz's sleigh. It didn't look like a pleasure trip. Franz's handsome face was serious and Holmes was staring straight ahead. Instead of turning up towards the forest at the end of the hotel drive they turned left for the village. Our walk also took us to the village because Father wanted to see an old man about getting a stick carved. When we walked down the little main street we saw the sleigh and horse standing outside a neat chalet with green shutters next to the church. I knew it was Franz's own house and wondered what had become of his passengers. About half an hour later, when we'd seen about Father's stick, we walked back up the street and there were Holmes and Watson standing on the balcony outside the chalet with Eva, the maid from last year. Her fair hair was as curly as ever but her head was bent. She seemed to be listening intently to something that Holmes was saying and the droop of her shoulders told me she wasn't happy.

'Why is Silver Stick talking to her?'

Amanda, very properly, was rebuked for staring and asking questions about things that didn't concern her. Being older and wiser, I said nothing but kept my secret coiled in my heart. Was it Eva who pushed him? Would they lock her up in prison? A little guilt stirred along with the pleasure, because he wouldn't have known about Eva if I hadn't told him, but not enough to spoil it. Later I watched from our window hoping to see the sleigh coming back, but it didn't that day. Instead, just before it got dark, Holmes and Watson came back on foot up the drive, walking fast, saying nothing.

Next morning, Square Bear came up to Mother at coffee time. 'I wonder if you would permit Miss Jessica to take a short walk with me on the terrace.'

Mother hesitated, but Square Bear was so obviously respectable, and anyway you could see the terrace from the coffee room. I put on my hat, cape and gloves and walked with him out of the glass doors into the cold air. We stood looking down at the rink, in exactly the same place as I'd been standing when they first spoke to me. I knew that was no accident. Square Bear's fussiness, the tension in his voice that he was so unsuccessful in hiding, left no doubt of it. There was something odd about the terrace too – far more people on it than would normally be the case on a cold morning. There must have been two dozen or so standing round in stiff little groups, talking to each other, waiting.

'Where's Mr Holmes?'

Square Bear looked at me, eyes watering from the cold.

'The truth is, my dear, I don't know where he is or what he's doing. He gave me my instructions at breakfast and I haven't seen him since.'

'Instructions about me?'

Before he could answer, the scream came. It was a man's scream, tearing through the air like a saw blade, and there was a word in it. The word was 'No'. I turned with the breath choking in my throat and, just as there'd been last year, there was a dark thing in the air, its clothes flapping out round it. A collective gasp from the people on the terrace, then a soft thump as the thing hit the deep snow on the restaurant roof and began sliding. I heard 'No' again, and this time it was my own voice, because I knew from last year what was coming next – the slide down the steep roof gathering snow as it came, the flop onto the terrace only a few yards from where I was standing, the arm sticking out.

At first the memory was so strong that I thought that was what I was seeing, and it took a few seconds for me to realise that it wasn't happening that way. The thing had fallen a little to the side and instead of sliding straight down the roof it was being carried to a little ornamental railing at the edge of it, where the main hotel joined onto the annex, driving a wedge of snow in front of it. Then somebody said, unbelievingly: 'He's stopped.' And the thing had stopped. Instead of plunging over the roof to the terrace, it had been swept up against the railing, bundled in snow like a cylindrical snow-ball and stopped within a yard of the edge. Then it sat up, clinging with one hand to the railing, covered from waist down in snow. If he'd been wearing a hat when he came out of the window he'd lost it in the fall because his damp hair was gleaming silver above his smiling brown face. It was an inward kind of smile, as if only he could appreciate the thing that he'd done.

Then the chattering started. Some people were yelling to get a ladder, others running. The rest were asking each other what had happened until somebody spotted the window wide open three floors above us.

'Her window. Mrs McEvoy's window.'

'He fell off Mrs McEvoy's balcony, just like last year.'

'But he didn't…'

At some point Square Bear had put a hand on my shoulder. Now he bent down beside me, looking anxiously into my face, saying we should go in and find Mother. I wished he'd get out of my way because I wanted to see Silver Stick on the roof. Then Mother arrived, wafting clouds of scent and drama. I had to go inside of course, but not before I'd seen the ladder arrive and Silver Stick coming down it, a little stiffly but dignified. And one more thing. Just as he stepped off the ladder the glass doors to the terrace opened and out she came. She hadn't been there when it happened but now, in her black fur jacket, she stepped through the people as if they weren't there, and gave him her hand and thanked him.

At dinner that night she dined alone at her table, as on the other nights, but it took her longer to get to it. Her long walk across the dining room was made longer by all the people who wanted to speak to her, to inquire after her health, to tell her how pleased they were to see her again. It was as if she'd just arrived that afternoon, instead of being there for five days already. There were several posies of flowers on her table that must have been sent up especially from the town, and champagne in a silver bucket beside it. Silver Stick and Square Bear bowed to her as she went past their table, but ordinary polite little nods, not like that first night. The smile she gave them was like the sun coming up.

We were sent off to bed as soon as we'd had our soup as usual. Amanda went to sleep at once but I lay awake, resenting my exile from what mattered. Our parents' sitting room was next to our bedroom and I heard them come in, excited still. Then, soon afterwards, a knock on the door of our suite, the murmur of voices and my father, a little taken aback, saying yes come in by all means. Then their voices, Square Bear's first, fussing with apologies about it being so late, then Silver Stick's cutting through him: 'The fact is, you're owed an explanation, or rather your daughter is. Dr Watson suggested that we should give it to you so that some time in the future when Jessica's old enough, you may decide to tell her.'

If I'd owned a chest of gold and had watched somebody throwing it away in a crowded street I couldn't have been more furious than hearing my secret about to be squandered. My first thought was to rush through to the other room in my night-dress and bare feet and demand that he should speak to me, not to them. Then caution took over, and although I did get out of bed, I went just as far as the door, opened it a crack so that I could hear better and padded back to bed. There were sounds of chairs being rearranged, people settling into them, then Silver Stick's voice.

'I should say at the start, for reasons we need not go into, that Dr Watson and I were convinced that Irene McEvoy had not pushed her husband to his death. The question was how to prove it, and in that regard your daughter's evidence was indispensable. She alone saw Mr McEvoy fall, and she alone heard what he shouted. The accurate ear of childhood – once certain adult nonsenses had been discarded – recorded that shout as precisely as a phonograph and knew that strictly speaking it was only half a shout, that Mr McEvoy, if he'd had time, would have added something else to it.'

A pause. I sat up in bed with the counterpane round my neck, straining not to miss a word of his quiet, clear voice.

'No – something. The question was, No what? Mr McEvoy had expected something to be there and his last thought on earth was surprise at the lack of it, surprise so acute that he was trying to shout it with his last breath. The question was, what that thing could have been.'

Silence, waiting for an answer, but nobody said anything.

'If you look up at the back of the hotel from the terrace you will notice one obvious thing. The third and fourth floors have balconies. The second floor does not. The room inhabited by Mr and Mrs McEvoy had a balcony. A person staying in the suite would be aware of that. He would not necessarily be aware, unless he were a particularly observant man, that the second-floor rooms had no balconies. Until it was too late. I formed the theory that Mr McEvoy had not in fact fallen from the window of his own room but from a

lower room belonging to somebody else, which accounted
for his attempted last words: "No ... balcony."'

My mother gasped. My father said: 'By Jove ...'

'Once I'd arrived at that conclusion, the question was
what Mr McEvoy was doing in somebody else's room. The
possibility of thieving could be ruled out since he was a very
rich man. Then he was seeing somebody. The next question
was who. And here your daughter was incidentally helpful in
a way she is too young to understand. She confided to us in
all innocence an overheard piece of adult gossip to the effect
that the late McEvoy had a roving eye.'

My father began to laugh, then stifled it. My mother said
'Well' in a way that boded trouble for me later.

'Once my attention was directed that way, the answer
became obvious. Mr McEvoy was in somebody else's hotel
room for what one might describe as an episode of *galanterie*.
But the accident happened in the middle of the morning.
Did ever a lady in the history of the world make a romantic
assignation for that hour of the day? Therefore it wasn't a
lady. So I asked myself what group of people are most likely
to be encountered in hotel rooms in mid-morning and the
answer was ...'

'Good heavens, the chambermaid.'

My mother's voice, and Holmes was clearly none too
pleased at being interrupted.

'Quite so. Mr McEvoy had gone to meet a chambermaid.
I asked some questions to establish whether any young and
attractive chambermaid had left the hotel since last Christmas. There was such a one, named Eva. She'd married the
under-porter and brought him as a dowry enough money

to buy that elegant little sleigh. Now a prudent chamber-maid may amass a modest dowry by saving tips, but one look at that sleigh will tell you that Eva's dowry might best be described as, well ... immodest.'

Another laugh from my father, cut off by a look from my mother I could well imagine.

'Dr Watson and I went to see Eva. I told her what I'd deduced and she, poor girl, confirmed it with some details – the sound of the housekeeper's voice outside, Mr McEvoy's well-practised but ill-advised tactic of taking refuge on the balcony. You may say that the girl Eva should have con-fessed at once what had happened ...'

'I do indeed.'

'But bear in mind her position. Not only her post at the hotel but her engagement to the handsome Franz would be forfeited. And, after all, there was no question of anybody being tried in court. The fashionable world was perfectly happy to connive at the story that Mr McEvoy had fallen accidentally from his window – while inwardly convicting an innocent woman of his murder.'

My mother said, sounding quite subdued for once: 'But Mrs McEvoy must have known. Why didn't she say something?'

'Ah, to answer that one needs to know something about Mrs McEvoy's history, and it so happens that Dr Watson and I are in that position. A long time ago, before her first happy marriage, Mrs McEvoy was loved by a prince. He was not, I must admit, a particularly admirable prince, but prince he was. Can you imagine how it felt for a woman to come from that to being deceived with a hotel chambermaid by a man who made his fortune from bathroom furnishings? Can you conceive that a proud woman might choose to be thought a murderess rather than submit to that indignity?'

Another silence, then my mother breathed: 'Yes. Yes, I think I can.' Then, 'Poor woman.'

'It was not pity that Irene McEvoy ever needed.' Then, in a different tone of voice: 'So there you have it. And it is your decision how much, if anything, you decide to pass on to Jessica in due course.'

There were sounds of people getting up from chairs, then my father said: 'And your, um, demonstration this morning?'

'Oh, that little drama. I knew what had happened, but for Mrs McEvoy's sake it was necessary to prove to the world she was innocent. I couldn't call Eva as witness because I'd given her my word. I'd studied the pitch of the roof and the depth of the snow and I was scientifically convinced that a man falling from Mrs McEvoy's balcony would not have landed on the terrace. You know the result.'

Good nights were said, rather subdued, and they were shown out. Through the crack in the door I glimpsed them. As they came level with the crack, Silver Stick, usually so precise in his movements, dropped his pipe and had to kneel to pick it up. As he knelt, his bright eyes met mine through the crack and he smiled, an odd, quick smile unseen by anybody else. He'd known I'd been listening all the time.

When they'd gone Mother and Father sat for a long time in silence.

At last Father said: 'If he'd got it wrong, he'd have killed himself.'

'Like the skiing.'

'He must have loved her very much.'
'It's his own logic he loves.'
But then, my mother always was the unromantic one.

Waxworks

Ethel Lina White

Sonia made her first entry in her notebook:

> Eleven o'clock. The lights are out. The porter has just locked
> the door. I can hear his footsteps echoing down the corridor.
> They grow fainter. Now there is silence. I am alone.

She stopped writing to glance at her company. Seen in the
light from the street-lamp, which streamed in through the
high window, the room seemed to be full of people. Their
faces were those of men and women of character and intelligence. They stood in groups, as though in conversation, or
sat apart, in solitary reverie.

But they neither moved nor spoke.

When Sonia had last seen them in the glare of the electric
globes, they had been a collection of ordinary waxworks,
some of which were the worse for wear. The black velvet

which lined the walls of the Gallery was alike tawdry and filmed with dust.

The side opposite to the window was built into alcoves, which held highly moral tableaux, depicting contrasting scenes in the career of Vice and Virtue. Sonia had slipped into one of these recesses, just before closing-time, in order to hide for her vigil.

It had been a simple affair. The porter had merely rung his bell, and the few courting-couples who represented the Public had taken his hint and hurried towards the exit.

No one was likely to risk being locked in, for the Waxwork Collection of Oldhampton had lately acquired a sinister reputation. The foundation for this lay in the fate of a stranger to the town – a commercial traveller – who had cut his throat in the Hall of Horrors.

Since then, two persons had, separately, spent the night in the Gallery and, in the morning, each had been found dead.

In both cases the verdict had been 'Natural death, due to heart failure.' The first victim – a local alderman – had been addicted to alcohol, and was in very bad shape. The second – his great friend – was a delicate little man, a martyr to asthma, and slightly unhinged through unwise absorption in spiritualism.

While the coincidence of the tragedies stirred up a considerable amount of local superstition, the general belief was that both deaths were due to the power of suggestion, in conjunction with macabre surroundings. The victims had let themselves be frightened to death by the Waxworks.

Sonia was there, in the Gallery, to test its truth.

She was the latest addition to the staff of the *Oldhampton*

Gazette. Bubbling with enthusiasm, she made no secret of her literary ambitions, and it was difficult to feed her with enough work. Her colleagues listened to her with mingled amusement and boredom, but they liked her as a refreshing novelty. As for her fine future, they looked to young Wells – the Sporting Editor – to effect her speedy and painless removal from the sphere of journalism.

On Christmas Eve, Sonia took them all into her confidence over her intention to spend a night in the Waxworks, on the last night of the old year.

'Copy there,' she declared. 'I'm not timid and I have fairly sensitive perceptions, so I ought to be able to write up the effect of imagination on the nervous system. I mean to record my impressions, every hour, while they're piping-hot.'

Looking up suddenly, she had surprised a green glare in the eyes of Hubert Poke.

When Sonia came to work on the *Gazette,* she had a secret fear of unwelcome amorous attentions, since she was the only woman on the staff. But the first passion she awoke was hatred.

Poke hated her impersonally, as the representative of a Force, numerically superior to his own sex, which was on the opposing side in the battle for existence. He feared her, too, because she was the unknown element, and possessed the unfair weapon of charm.

Before she came, he had been the star turn on the *Gazette.* His own position on the staff gratified his vanity and entirely satisfied his narrow ambition. But Sonia had stolen some of his thunder. On more than one occasion she had written up a story he had failed to cover, and he had to admit that her success was due to a quicker wit.

For some time past he had been playing with the idea of spending a night in the Waxworks, but was deterred by the knowledge that his brain was not sufficiently temperate for the experiment. Lately he had been subject to sudden red rages, when he had felt a thick hot taste in his throat, as though of blood. He knew that his jealousy of Sonia was accountable. It had almost reached the stage of mania, and trembled on the brink of homicidal urge.

While his brain was still creaking with the idea of first-hand experience in the ill-omened Gallery, Sonia had nipped in with her ready-made plan.

Controlling himself with an effort, he listened while the sub-editor issued a warning to Sonia.

'Bon idea, young woman, but you will find the experience a bit raw. You've no notion how uncanny these big deserted buildings can be.'

'That's so,' nodded young Wells. 'I once spent a night in a haunted house.'

Sonia looked at him with her habitual interest. He was short and thick-set, with a three-cornered smile which appealed to her.

'Did you see anything?' she asked.

'No, I cleared out before the show came on. Windy. After a bit, one can imagine *anything*.'

It was then that Poke introduced a new note into the discussion by his own theory of the mystery deaths.

Sitting alone in the deserted Gallery, Sonia preferred to forget his words. She resolutely drove them from her mind while she began to settle down for the night.

Her first action was to cross to the figure of Cardinal

Wolsey and unceremoniously raise his heavy scarlet robe. From under its voluminous folds, she drew out her cushion and attaché-case, which she had hidden earlier in the evening.

Mindful of the fact that it would grow chilly at dawn, she carried on her arm her thick white tennis-coat. Slipping it on, she placed her cushion in the angle of the wall, and sat down to await developments.

The Gallery was far more mysterious now that the lights were out. At either end, it seemed to stretch away into impenetrable black tunnels. But there was nothing uncanny about it, or about the figures, which were a tame and conventional collection of historical personages. Even the adjoining Hall of Horrors contained no horrors, only a selection of respectable-looking poisoners.

Sonia grinned cheerfully at the row of waxworks which were visible in the lamplight from the street.

'So you are the villains of the piece,' she murmured. 'Later on, if the office is right, you will assume unpleasant mannerisms to try to cheat me into believing you are alive. I warn you, old sports, you'll have your work cut out for you … And now I think I'll get better acquainted with you. Familiarity breeds contempt.'

She went the round of the figures, greeting each with flippancy or criticism. Presently she returned to her corner and opened her note-book ready to record her impressions.

Twelve o'clock. The first hour has passed almost too quickly. I've drawn a complete blank. Not a blessed thing to record. Not a vestige of reaction. The waxworks seem a commonplace lot, without a scrap of hypnotic force. In fact, they're altogether too matey.

Sonia had left her corner, to write her entry in the light which streamed through the window. Smoking was prohibited in the building, and, lest she should yield to temptation, she had left both her cigarettes and matches behind her, on the office table.

At this stage she regretted the matches. A little extra light would be a boon. It was true she carried an electric torch, but she was saving it, in case of emergency.

It was a loan from young Wells. As they were leaving the office together, he spoke to her confidentially.

'Did you notice how Poke glared at you? Don't get up against him. He's a nasty piece of work. He's so mean he'd sell his mother's shroud for old rags. And he's a cruel little devil, too. He turned out his miserable pup, to starve in the streets, rather than cough up for the license.'

Sonia grew hot with indignation.

'What he needs to cure his complaint is a strong dose of rat-poison,' she declared. 'What became of the poor little dog?'

'Oh, he's all right. He was a matey chap, and he soon chummed up with a mongrel of his own class.'

'You?' asked Sonia, her eyes suddenly soft.

'A mongrel, am I?' grinned Wells. 'Well, anyway, the pup will get a better Christmas than his first, when Poke went away and left him on the chain . ... We're both of us going to over-eat and over-drink. You're on your own, too. Won't you join us?'

'I'd love to.'

Although the evening was Warm and muggy the invitation suffused Sonia with the spirit of Christmas. The shade of Dickens seemed to be hovering over the parade of the streets. A red-nosed Santa Claus presided over a spangled Christmas-tree outside a toy-shop. Windows were hung with tinselled balls and coloured paper festoons. Pedestrians, laden with parcels, called out seasonable greetings.

'Merry Christmas.'

Young Wells's three-cornered smile was his tribute to the joyous feeling of festival. His eyes were eager as he turned to Sonia.

'I've an idea. Don't wait until after the holidays to write up the Waxworks. Make it a Christmas stunt, and go there tonight.'

'I will,' declared Sonia.

It was then that he slipped the torch into her hand.

'I know you belong to the stronger sex,' he said. 'But even your nerve might crash. If it does, just flash this torch under the window. Stretch out your arm above your head, and the light will be seen from the street.'

'And what will happen then?' asked Sonia.

'I shall knock up the miserable porter and let you out.'

'But how will *you* see the light?'

'I shall be in the street.'

'All night?'

'Yes; I sleep there.' Young Wells grinned. 'Understand,' he added loftily, 'that this is a matter of principle. I could not let any woman – even one so aged and unattractive as yourself – feel beyond the reach of help.'

He cut into her thanks as he turned away with a parting warning.

'Don't use the torch for light, or the juice may give out. It's about due for a new battery.'

As Sonia looked at the torch, lying by her side, it seemed a link with young Wells. At this moment he was patrolling the street, a sturdy figure in an old tweed overcoat, with his cap pulled down over his eyes.

As she tried to pick out his footsteps from among those of the other passers-by, it struck her that there was plenty of traffic, considering that it was past twelve o'clock.

'The witching hour of midnight is another lost illusion,' she reflected. 'Killed by night-clubs, I suppose.'

It was cheerful to know that so many citizens were abroad, to keep her company. Some optimists were still singing carols. She faintly heard the strains of 'Good King Wenceslas.' It was in a tranquil frame of mind that she unpacked her sandwiches and thermos.

'It's Christmas Day,' she thought, as she drank hot coffee. 'And I'm spending it with Don and the pup.'

At that moment her career grew misty, and the flame of her literary ambition dipped as the future glowed with the warm firelight of home. In sudden elation, she held up her flask and toasted the waxworks.

'Merry Christmas to you all! And many of them.'

The faces of the illuminated figures remained stolid, but she could almost swear that a low murmur of acknowledgment seemed to swell from the rest of her company – invisible in the darkness.

She spun out her meal to its limit, stifling her craving for a cigarette. Then, growing bored, she counted the visible waxworks, and tried to memorise them.

'Twenty-one, twenty-two … Wolsey. Queen Elizabeth, Guy Fawkes, Napoleon ought to go on a diet. Ever heard of eighteen days, Nap? Poor old Julius Caesar looks as though he'd been sun-bathing on the Lido. He's about due for the melting-pot.'

In her eyes they were a second-rate set of dummies. The local theory that they could terrorise a human being to death or madness seemed a fantastic notion.

'No,' concluded Sonia. 'There's really more in Poke's bright idea.'

Again she saw the sun-smitten office – for the big unshielded window faced south – with its blistered paint, faded wall-paper, ink-stained desks, typewriters, telephones, and a huge fire in the untidy grate. Young Wells smoked his big pipe, while the sub-editor – a ginger, pig-headed young man – laid down the law about the mystery deaths.

And then she heard Poke's toneless deadman's voice.

'You may be right about the spiritualist. He died of fright – but not of the waxworks. My belief is that he established contacrwith the spirit of his dead friend, the alderman, and so learned his real fate.'

'What fate?' snapped the sub-editor.

'I believe that the alderman was murdered,' replied Poke.

He clung to his point like a limpet in the face of all counter-arguments.

'The alderman had enemies,' he said. 'Nothing would be easier than for one of them to lie in wait for him. In the present circumstances, *I* could commit a murder in the Wax-works, and get away with it.'

'How?' demanded young Wells.

'How? To begin with, the Gallery is a one-man show and the porter's a bone-head. Anyone could enter, and leave, the Gallery without his being wise to it.'

'And the murder?' plugged young Wells.

With a shudder Sonia remembered how Poke had glanced at his long, knotted fingers.

'If I could not achieve my object by fright, which is the foolproof way,' he replied, 'I should try a little artistic strangulation.'

'And leave your marks?'

'Not necessarily. Every expert knows that there are methods which show no trace.'

Sonia fumbled in her bag for the cigarettes which were not there.

'Why did I let myself think of that, just now?' she thought. 'Really too stupid.'

As she reproached herself for her morbidity, she broke off to stare at the door which led to the Hall of Horrors.

When she had last looked at it, she could have sworn that it was tightly closed ... But now it gaped open by an inch.

She looked at the black cavity, recognizing the first test of her nerves. Later on, there would be others. She realized the fact that, within her cool, practical self, she carried a hysterical, neurotic passenger, who would doubtless give her a lot of trouble through officious suggestions and uncomfortable reminders.

She resolved to give her second self a taste of her quality, and so quell her at the start.

'That door was merely closed,' she remarked as, with a firm step, she crossed to the Hall of Horrors and shut the door.

One o'clock. I begin to realize that there is more in this than I thought. Perhaps I'm missing my sleep. But I'm keyed up and horribly expectant. Of what? I don't know. But I seem to be waiting for – something. I find myself listening – listening. The place is full of mysterious noises. I know they're my fancy .. .And things appear to move. Lean distinguish footsteps and whispers, as though those waxworks which I cannot see in the darkness are beginning to stir to life.

Sonia dropped her pencil at the sound of a low chuckle. It seemed to come from the end of the Gallery which was blacked out by shadows.

As her imagination galloped away with her, she reproached herself sharply.

'Steady, don't be a fool. There must be a cloak-room here. That chuckle is the air escaping in a pipe – or something. I'm betrayed by my own ignorance of hydraulics.'

In spite of her brave words, she returned rather quickly to her corner.

With her back against the wall she felt less apprehensive. But she recognized her cowardice as an ominous sign.

She was desperately afraid of someone – or something – creeping up behind her and touching her.

'I've struck the bad patch,' she told herself. 'It will be worse at three o'clock and work up to a climax. But when I make my entry, at three, I shall have reached the peak. After that every minute will be bringing the dawn nearer.'

But of one fact she was ignorant. There would be no recorded impression at three o'clock.

Happily unconscious, she began to think of her copy.

When she returned to the office – sunken-eyed, and looking like nothing on earth – she would then rejoice over every symptom of groundless fear.

'It's a story all right,' she gloated, looking at Hamlet. His gnarled, pallid features and dark, smouldering eyes were strangely familiar to her.

Suddenly she realized that he reminded her of Hubert Poke.

Against her will, her thoughts again turned to him. She told herself that he was exactly like a waxwork. His yellow face – symptomatic of heart-trouble – had the same cheesy hue, and his eyes were like dull black glass. He wore a denture which was too large for him, and which forced his lips apart in a mirthless grin.

He always seemed to smile – even over the episode of the lift – which had been no joke.

It happened two days before. Sonia had rushed into the office in a state of molten excitement because she had extracted an interview from a Personage who had just received the Freedom of the City. This distinguished freeman had the reputation of shunning newspaper publicity, and Poke had tried his luck, only to be sent away with a flea in his ear.

At the back of her mind, Sonia knew that she had not fought level, for she was conscious of the effect of violet-blue eyes and a dimple upon a reserved but very human gentleman. But in her elation she had been rather blatant about her score.

She transcribed her notes, rattling away at her typewriter in a tremendous hurry, because she had a dinner-engagement. In the same breathless speed she had rushed towards the automatic lift.

She was just about to step into it when young Wells had leaped the length of the passage and dragged her back.

'Look, where you're going!' he shouted.

Sonia looked – and saw only the well of the shaft. The lift was not waiting in its accustomed place.

'Out of order,' explained Wells before he turned to blast Hubert Poke, who stood by.

'You almighty chump, why didn't you grab Miss Fraser, instead of standing by like a stuck pig?'

At the time Sonia had vaguely remarked how Poke had stammered and sweated, and she accepted the fact that he had been petrified by shock and had lost his head.

For the first time, she realized that his inaction had been deliberate. She remembered the flame of terrible excitement in his eyes and his stretched ghastly grin.

'He *hates* me,' she thought. 'It's my fault. I've been tactless and cocksure.'

Then a flood of horror swept over her.

'But he wanted to see me crash. It's almost *murder*.'

As she began to tremble, the jumpy passenger she carried reminded her of Poke's remark about the alderman.

'He had enemies.'

Sonia shook away the suggestion angrily.

'My memory's uncanny,' she thought. 'I'm stimulated and all strung up. It must be the atmosphere … Perhaps there's some gas in the air that accounts for these brainstorms. It's hopeless to be so utterly unscientific. Poke would have made a better job of this.'

She was back again to Hubert Poke. He had become an obsession.

Her head began to throb and a tiny gong started to beat in her temples. This time, she recognized the signs without any mental ferment.

'Atmospherics. A storm's coming up. It might make things rather thrilling. I must concentrate on my story. Really, my luck's in.'

She sat for some time, forcing herself to think of pleasant subjects – of arguments with young Wells and the Tennis Tournament. But there was always a point when her thoughts gave a twist and led her back to Poke.

Presently she grew cramped and got up to pace the illuminated aisle in front of the window. She tried again to talk to the waxworks, but, this time, it was not a success.

They seemed to have grown remote and secretive, as though they were removed to another plane, where they possessed a hidden life.

Suddenly she gave a faint scream. Someone – or something – had crept up behind her, for she felt the touch of cold fingers upon her arm.

Two o'clock. They're only wax. They shall not frighten me. But they're trying to. One by one they're coming to life .. . Charles the Second no longer looks sour dough. He is beginning to leer at me. His eyes remind me of Hubert Poke.

Sonia stopped writing, to glance uneasily at the image of the Stuart monarch. His black velveteen suit appeared to have a richer pile. The swart curls which fell over his lace collar looked less like horse-hair. There really seemed a gleam of amorous interest lurking at the back of his glass optics.

Absurdly, Sonia spoke to him, in order to reassure herself.

'Did *you* touch me? At the first hint of a liberty, Charles Stuart, I'll smack your face. You'll learn a modern journalist has not the manners of an orange-girl.'

Instantly the satyr reverted to a dummy in a moth-eaten historical costume.

Sonia stood, listening for young Wells's footsteps. But she could not hear them, although the street now was perfectly still. She tried to picture him, propping up the opposite building, solid and immovable as the Rock of Gibraltar.

But it was no good. Doubts began to obtrude.

'I don't believe he's there. After all, why should he stay? He only pretended, just to give me confidence. He's gone.'

She shrank back to her corner, drawing her tennis-coat closer, for warmth. It was growing colder, causing her to think of tempting things – of a hot-water bottle and a steaming tea-pot.

Presently she realized that she was growing drowsy. Her lids felt as though weighted with lead, so that it required an effort to keep them open.

This was a complication which she had not foreseen. Although she longed to drop off to sleep, she sternly resisted the temptation.

'No. It's not fair. I've set myself the job of recording a night spent in the Waxworks. It *must* be the genuine thing.'

She blinked more vigorously, staring across to where Byron drooped like a sooty flamingo.

'Mercy, how he yearns! He reminds me of ... No, I won't

think of *him* … I must keep awake … Bed … blankets, pillows … No.'

Her head fell forward, and for a minute she dozed. In that space of time, she had a vivid dream.

She thought that she was still in her corner in the Gallery, watching the dead alderman as he paced to and fro, before the window. She had never seen him, so he conformed to her own idea of an alderman – stout, pompous, and wearing the dark-blue, fur-trimmed robe of his office.

'He's got a face like a sleepy pear,' she decided. 'Nice old thing, but brainless.'

And then, suddenly, her tolerant derision turned to acute apprehension on his account, as she saw that he was being followed. A shape was stalking him as a cat stalks a bird.

Sonia tried to warn him of his peril, but, after the fashion of nightmares, she found herself voiceless. Even as she struggled to scream, a grotesquely long arm shot out and monstrous fingers gripped the alderman's throat.

In the same moment, she saw the face of the killer. It was Hubert Poke.

She awoke with a start, glad to find that it was but a dream. As she looked around her with dazed eyes, she saw a faint flicker of light. The mutter of very faint thunder, together with a patter of rain, told her that the storm had broken.

It was still a long way off, for Oldhampton seemed to be having merely a reflection and an echo.

'It'll clear the air,' thought Sonia.

Then her heart gave a violent leap. One of the waxworks had come to life. She distinctly saw it move, before it disappeared into the darkness at the end of the Gallery.

She kept her head, realizing that it was time to give up.

'My nerve's crashed,' she thought. 'That figure was only my fancy. I'm just like the others. Defeated by wax.'

Instinctively, she paid the figures her homage. It was the cumulative effect of their grim company, with their simulated life and sinister associations, that had rushed her defences. Although it was bitter to fail, she comforted herself with the reminder that she had enough copy for her article. She could even make capital out of her own capitulation to the force of suggestion.

With a slight grimace, she picked up her notebook. There would be no more on-the-spot impressions. But young Wells, if he was still there, would be grateful for the end of his vigil, whatever the state of mind of the porter.

She groped in the darkness for her signal-lamp. But her fingers only scraped bare polished boards.

The torch had disappeared.

In a panic, she dropped down on her knees, and searched for yards around the spot where she was positive it had lain.

It was the instinct of self-preservation which caused her to give up her vain search.

'I'm in danger,' she thought. 'And I've no one to help me now. I must see this through myself.'

She pushed back her hair from a brow which had grown damp.

'There's a brain working against mine. When I was asleep, someone – or something – stole my torch.'

Something? The waxworks became instinct with terrible possibility as she stared at them. Some were merely blurred shapes – their faces opaque oblongs or ovals. But others – illuminated from the street – were beginning to reveal themselves in a new guise.

Queen Elizabeth, with peaked chin and fiery hair, seemed to regard her with intelligent malice. The countenance of Napoléon was heavy with brooding power, as though he were willing her to submit. Cardinal Wolsey held her with a glittering eye.

Sonia realized that she was letting herself be hypnotised by creatures of wax – so many pounds of candles moulded to human form.

'This is what happened to those others,' she thought. *'Nothing happened.* But I'm afraid of them. I'm terribly afraid . ... There's only one thing to do. I must count them again.'

She knew that she must find out whether her torch had been stolen through human agency; but she shrank from the experiment, not knowing which she feared more – a tangible enemy or the unknown.

As she began to count, the chilly air inside the building seemed to throb with each thud of her heart.

'Seventeen, eighteen.' She was scarcely conscious of the numerals she murmured. 'Twenty-two, twenty-three.'

She stopped. Twenty-three? If her tally were correct, there was an extra waxwork in the Gallery.

On the shock of the discovery came a blinding flash of light, which veined the sky with fire. It seemed to run down the figure of Joan of Arc like a flaming torch. By a freak of atmospherics, the storm, which had been a starved, whimpering affair of flicker and murmur, culminated, and ended, in what was apparently a thunderbolt.

The explosion which followed was stunning; but Sonia scarcely noticed it, in her terror. The unearthly violet glare had revealed to her a figure which she had previously overlooked.

It was seated in a chair, its hand supporting its peaked chin, and its pallid, clean-shaven features nearly hidden by a familiar broad-brimmed felt hat, which – together with the black cape – gave her the clue to its identity.

It was Hubert Poke.

Three o'clock.
Sonia heard it strike, as her memory began to reproduce, with horrible fidelity, every word of Poke's conversation on murder.

'Artistic strangulation.' She pictured the cruel agony of life leaking – bubble by bubble, gasp by gasp. It would be slow – for he had boasted of a method which left no tell-tale marks.

'Another death,' she thought dully. 'If it happens every-one will say that the Waxworks have killed me. What a story … Only, I shall not write it up.'

The tramp of feet rang out on the pavement below. It might have been the policeman on his beat; but Sonia wanted to feel that young Wells was still faithful to his post.

She looked up at the window, set high in the wall, and, for a moment, was tempted to shout. But the idea was too desperate. If she failed to attract outside attention, she would seal her own fate, for Poke would be prompted to hasten her extinction.

'Awful to feel he's so near, and yet I cannot reach him,' she thought. 'It makes it so much worse.'

She crouched there, starting and sweating at every faint sound in the darkness. The rain, which still pattered on the sky-light, mimicked footsteps and whispers. She remembered her dream and the nightmare spring and clutch.

It was an omen. At any moment it would come ...

Her fear jolted her brain. For the first time she had a glimmer of hope.

'I didn't see him before the flash, because he looked exactly like one of the waxworks. Could I hide among them, too?' she wondered.

She knew that her white coat alone revealed her position to him. Holding her breath, she wriggled out of it, and hung it on the effigy of Charles II. In her black coat, with her handkerchief-scarf tied over her face, burglar fashion, she hoped that she was invisible against the sable-draped walls.

Her knees shook as she crept from her shelter. When she had stolen a few yards, she stopped to listen ... In the darkness, someone was astir. She heard a soft padding of feet, moving with the certainty of one who sees his goal.

Her coat glimmered in her deserted corner.

In a sudden panic, she increased her pace, straining her ears for other sounds. She had reached the far end of the Gallery where no gleam from the window penetrated the gloom. Blindfolded and muffled, she groped her way towards the akoves which held the tableaux.

Suddenly she stopped, every nerve in her body quivering.

She had heard a thud, like rubbered soles alighting after a spring.

'He knows now.' Swift on the trail of her thought flashed another. 'He will look for me. Oh, *quick!*'

She tried to move, but her muscles were bound, and she stood as though rooted to the spot, listening. It was impossible to locate the footsteps. They seemed to come from every quarter of the Gallery. Sometimes they sounded remote, but, whenever she drew a freer breath, a sudden creak of the boards close to where she stood made her heart leap.

At last she reached the limit of endurance. Unable to bear the suspense of waiting, she moved on.

Her pursuer followed her at a distance. He gained on her, but still withheld his spring. She had the feeling that he held her at the end of an invisible string.

'He's playing with me, like a cat with a mouse,' she thought.

If he had seen her, he let her creep forward until the darkness was no longer absolute. There were gradations in its density, so that she was able to recognize the first alcove. Straining her eyes, she could distinguish the outlines of the bed where the Virtuous Man made his triumphant exit from life, surrounded by a flock of his sorrowing family and their progeny.

Slipping inside the circle, she added one more mourner to the tableau.

The minutes passed, but nothing happened. There seemed no sound save the tiny gong beating inside her temples. Even the raindrops had ceased to patter on the sky-light. Sonia began to find the silence more deadly than noise. It was like the lull before the storm. Question after question came rolling into her mind.

'Where is he? What will he do next? Why doesn't he strike a light?'

As though someone were listening-in to her thoughts, she suddenly heard a faint splutter as of an ignited match. Or it might have been the click of an exhausted electric torch.

With her back turned to the 'room, she could see no light. She heard the half-hour strike, with a faint wonder that she was still alive.

'What will have happened before the next quarter?' she asked.

Presently she began to feel the strain of her pose, which she held as rigidly as any artist's model. For the time – if her presence were not already detected – her life depended on her immobility.

As an overpowering weariness began to steal over her a whisper stirred in her brain:

'The alderman was found dead on a bed.'

The newspaper account had not specified which especial tableau had been the scene of the tragedy, but she could not remember another alcove which held a bed. As she stared at the white dimness of the quilt she seemed to see it blotched with a dark, sprawling form, writhing under the grip of long fingers.

To shut out the suggestion of her fancy, she closed her eyes. The cold, dead air in the alcove was sapping her exhausted vitality, so that once again she began to nod. She dozed as she stood, rocking to and fro on her feet.

Her surroundings grew shadowy. Sometimes she knew that she was in the alcove, but at others she strayed momentarily over strange borders ... She was back in the summer, walking in a garden with young Wells. Roses and sunshine ...

She awoke with a start at the sound of heavy breathing. It sounded close to her – almost by her side. The figure of a mourner kneeling by the bed seemed to change its posture slightly.

Instantly maddened thoughts began to flock and flutter wildly inside her brain.

'Who was it? Was it Hubert Poke? Would history be repeated? Was she doomed also to be strangled inside the alcove? Had Fate led her there?'

She waited, but nothing happened. Again she had the sensation of being played with by a master mind – dangled at the end of his invisible string.

Presently she was emboldened to steal from the alcove, to seek another shelter. But though she held on to the last flicker of her will, she had reached the limit of endurance. Worn out with the violence of her emotions and physically spent from the strain of long periods of standing, she staggered as she walked.

She blundered round the Gallery, without any sense of direction, colliding blindly with the groups of waxwork figures. When she reached the window her knees shook under her and she sank to the ground – dropping immediately into a sleep of utter exhaustion.

She awoke with a start as the first grey gleam of dawn was stealing into the Gallery. It fell on the row of waxworks, imparting a sickly hue to their features, as though they were creatures stricken with plague.

It seemed to Sonia that they were waiting for her to wake. Their peaked faces were intelligent and their eyes held interest, as though they were keeping some secret.

She pushed back her hair, her brain still thick with clouded memories. Disconnected thoughts began to stir, to slide about.. . Then suddenly her mind cleared, and she sprang up – staring at a figure wearing a familiar black cape.

Hubert Poke was also waiting for her to wake.

He sat in the same chair, and in the same posture, as when she had first seen him, in the flash of lightning. He looked as though he had never moved from his place – as though he could not move. His face had not the appearance of flesh.

As Sonia stared at him, with the feeling of a bird hypnotised by a snake, a doubt began to gather in her mind. Growing bolder, she crept closer to the figure.

It was a waxwork – a libellous representation of the actor – Kean.

Her laugh rang joyously through the Gallery as she realized that she had passed a night of baseless terrors, cheated by the power of imagination. In her relief she turned impulsively to the waxworks.

'My congratulations,' she said. 'You are my masters.'

They did not seem entirely satisfied by her homage, for they continued to watch her with an expression half-benevolent and half-sinister.

'*Wait!*' they seemed to say.

Sonia turned from them and opened her bag to get out her

mirror and comb. There, among a jumble of notes, letters, lipsticks, and powder-compresses, she saw the electric torch.

'*Of course!*' she cried. 'I remember now, I put it there. I was too windy to think properly … Well, I have my story. I'd better get my coat.'

The Gallery seemed smaller in the returning light. As she approached Charles Stuart, who looked like an umpire in her white coat, she glanced down the far end of the room, where she had groped in its shadows before the pursuit of imaginary footsteps.

A waxwork was lying prone on the floor. For the second time she stood and gazed down upon a familiar black cape – a broad-brimmed conspirator's hat. Then she nerved herself to turn the figure so that its face was visible.

She gave a scream. There was no mistaking the glazed eyes and ghastly grin. She was looking down on the face of a dead man.

It was Hubert Poke.

The shock was too much for Sonia. She heard a singing in her ears, while a black mist gathered before her eyes. For the first time in her life she fainted.

When she recovered consciousness she forced herself to kneel beside the body and cover it with its black cape. The pallid face resembled a death-mask, which revealed only too plainly the lines of egotism and cruelty in which it had been moulded by a gross spirit.

Yet Sonia felt no repulsion – only pity. It was Christmas morning, and he was dead, while her own portion was life triumphant. Closing her eyes, she whispered a prayer of supplication for his warped soul.

Presently, as she grew calmer, her mind began to work on the problem of his presence. His motive seemed obvious. Not knowing that she had changed her plan, he had concealed himself in the Gallery, in order to poach her story.

'He was in the Hall of Horrors at first,' she thought, remembering the opened door. 'When he came out he hid at this end. We never saw each other, because of the waxworks between us; but we heard each other.'

She realized that the sounds which had terrified her had not all been due to imagination, while it was her agency which had converted the room into a whispering gallery of strange murmurs and voices. The clue to the cause of death was revealed by his wrist-watch, which had smashed when he fell. Its hands had stopped at three minutes to three, proving that the flash and explosion of the thunderbolt had been too much for his diseased heart – already overstrained by superstitious fears.

Sonia shuddered at a mental vision of his face, distraught with terror and pulped by raw primal impulses, after a night spent in a madman's world of phantasy.

She turned to look at the waxworks. At last she understood what they seemed to say.

'But for Us, you should have met – at dawn.'

'Your share shall be acknowledged, I promise you,' she said, as she opened her notebook.

Eight o'clock. The Christmas bells are ringing and it is wonderful just to be alive. I'm through the night, and none the worse for the experience, although I cracked badly after three o'clock. A colleague who, unknown to me, was also concealed in the Gallery has met with a tragic fate, caused, I am sure, by the force of suggestion. Although his death is due to heart-failure, the superstitious will certainly claim it is another victory for the Waxworks.

Twixt the Cup and the Lip

Julian Symons

'Beautiful morning, Miss Oliphant. I shall take a short constitutional.'

'Very well, Mr Payne.'

Mr Rossiter Payne put on his good thick Melton overcoat, took his bowler hat off its peg, carefully brushed it and put it on. He looked at himself in a small glass and nodded approvingly at what he saw.

He was a man in his early fifties, but he might have passed for ten years less, so square were his shoulders, so ruler-straight his back. Two fine wings of grey hair showed under the bowler. He looked like a retired Guards officer, although he had, in fact, no closer relationship with the Army than an uncle who had been cashiered.

At the door he paused, his eyes twinkling. 'Don't let anybody steal the stock while I'm out, Miss Oliphant.'

Miss Oliphant, a thin spinster of indeterminate middle age, blushed. She adored Mr Payne.

He had removed his hat to speak to her. Now he clapped it on his head again, cast an appreciative look at the bow window of his shop, which displayed several sets of standard authors with the discreet legend above – *Rossiter Payne, Bookseller. Specialist in First Editions and Manuscripts* – and made his way up New Bond Street towards Oxford Street.

At the top of New Bond Street he stopped, as he did five days a week, at the stall on the corner. The old woman put the carnation into his buttonhole.

'Fourteen shopping days to Christmas now, Mrs Shankly. We've all got to think about it, haven't we?'

A ten shilling note changed hands instead of the usual half crown. He left her blessing him confusedly.

This was perfect December weather – crisply cold, the sun shining. Oxford Street was wearing its holiday decorations – enormous gold and silver coins from which depended ropes of pearls, diamonds, rubies, emeralds. When lighted up in the afternoon they looked pretty, although a little garish for Mr Payne's refined taste. But still, they had a certain symbolic feeling about them, and he smiled at them.

Nothing, indeed, could disturb Mr Payne's good temper this morning – not the jostling crowds on the pavements or the customary traffic jams, which seemed, indeed, to please him. He walked along until he came to a large store that said above it, in enormous letters, ORBIN'S. These letters were picked out in coloured lights, and the lights themselves were festooned with Christmas trees and holly wreaths and the figures of the Seven Dwarfs, all of which lighted up.

Orbin's department store went right round the corner into the comparatively quiet Jessiter Street. Once again Mr Payne went through a customary ceremony. He crossed the road and went down several steps into an establishment unique of its kind – Danny's Shoe Parlour. Here, sitting on a kind of throne in this semi-basement, one saw through a small window the lower halves of passers-by. Here Danny, with two assistants almost as old as himself, had been shining shoes for almost thirty years.

Leather-faced, immensely lined but still remarkably sharp-eyed, Danny knelt down now in front of Mr Payne, turned up the cuffs of his trousers and began to put an altogether superior shine on already well-polished shoes.

'Lovely morning, Mr Payne.'

'You can't see much of it from here.'

'More than you think. You see the pavements, and if they're not spotted, right off you know it isn't raining. Then there's something in the way people walk, you know what I mean, like it's Christmas in the air.' Mr Payne laughed indulgently. Now Danny was mildly reproachful. 'You still haven't brought me in that pair of black shoes, sir.'

Mr Payne frowned slightly. A week ago he had been almost knocked down by a bicyclist, and the mudguard of the bicycle had scraped badly one of the shoes he was wearing, cutting the leather at one point. Danny was confident that he could repair the cut so that it wouldn't show. Mr Payne was not so sure.

'I'll bring them along,' he said vaguely.

'Sooner the better, Mr Payne, sooner the better.'

Mr Payne did not like being reminded of the bicycle incident. He gave Danny half a crown instead of the ten shillings he had intended, crossed the road again and walked into the side entrance of Orbin's, which called itself unequivocally 'London's Greatest Department Store'.

This end of the store was quiet. He walked up the stairs, past the grocery department on the ground floor, and wine and cigars on the second, to jewellery on the third. There were rarely many people in this department, but today a small crowd had gathered around a man who was making a speech. A placard at the department entrance said: 'The Russian Royal Family Jewels. On display for two weeks by kind permission of the Grand Duke and Grand Duchess of Moldo-Lithuania.'

These were not the Russian Crown Jewels, seized by the Bolsheviks during the Revolution, but an inferior collection brought out of Russia by the Grand Duke and Grand Duchess, who had long since become plain Mr and Mrs Skandorski, who lived in New Jersey and were now on a visit to England.

Mr Payne was not interested in Mr and Mrs Skandorski, or in Sir Henry Orbin, who was stumbling through a short speech. He was interested only in the jewels. When the speech was over he mingled with the crowd round the showcase that stood almost in the middle of the room.

The royal jewels lay on beds of velvet – a tiara that looked too heavy to be worn, diamond necklaces and bracelets, a cluster of diamonds and emeralds, and a dozen other pieces, each with an elegant calligraphic description of its origin and history. Mr Payne did not see the jewels as a romantic relic of the past, nor did he permit himself to think of them as things of beauty. He saw them as his personal Christmas present.

He walked out of the department, looking neither to left nor right, and certainly paying no attention to the spotty young clerk who rushed forward to open the door for him. He walked back to his bookshop, sniffing that sharp December air, made another little joke to Miss Oliphant and told her she could go out to lunch. During her lunch hour he sold an American a set of a Victorian magazine called *The Jewel Box*.

It seemed a good augury.

In the past ten years Mr Payne had engineered successfully – with the help of other, and inferior, intellects – six jewel robberies. He had remained undetected, he believed, partly because of his skill in planning, partly because he ran a perfectly legitimate book business and partly because he broke the law only when he needed money. He had little interest in women, and his habits were generally ascetic, but he did have one vice.

Mr Payne developed a system at roulette, an improvement on the almost infallible Frank-Konig system, and every year he went to Monte Carlo and played his system. Almost every year it failed – or rather, it revealed certain imperfections, which he then tried to remedy.

It was to support his foolproof system that Mr Payne had turned from bookselling to crime. He believed himself to be, in a quiet way, a mastermind in the modern criminal world.

Those associated with him were far from that, as he immediately would have acknowledged. He met them two evenings after he had looked at the royal jewels, in his pleasant little flat above the shop, which could be approached from a side entrance opening into an alley.

There was Stacey, who looked what he was, a thick-nosed thug; there was a thin young man in a tight suit whose name was Jack Line, and who was always called Straight or Straight Line; and there was Lester Jones, the spotty clerk in the Jewellery Department.

Stacey and Straight Line sat drinking whisky, Mr Payne sipped some excellent sherry and Lester Jones drank nothing at all, while Mr Payne in his pedantic, almost schoolmasterly manner told them how the robbery was to be accomplished.

'You all know what the job is, but let me tell you how much it is worth. In its present form the collection is worth whatever sum you'd care to mention – a quarter of a million pounds perhaps. There is no real market value. But alas, it will have to be broken up. My friend thinks the value will be in the neighbourhood of fifty thousand pounds. Not less, and not much more.'

'Your friend?' the jewellery clerk said timidly.

'The fence. Lambie, isn't it?' It was Stacey who spoke. Mr Payne nodded. 'Okay, how do we split?'

'I will come to that later. Now, here are the difficulties. First of all, there are two store detectives on each floor. We must see to it that those on the third floor are not in the Jewellery Department. Next, there is a man named Davidson, an American, whose job it is to keep an eye on the jewels. He has been brought over here by a protection agency and it is likely that he will carry a gun. Third, the jewels are in a showcase, and any attempt to open this showcase other than with the proper key will set off an alarm. The key is kept in the Manager's Office, inside the Jewellery Department.'

Stacey got up, shambled over to the whisky decanter, and poured himself another drink. 'Where do you get all this from?'

Mr Payne permitted himself a small smile. 'Lester works in the department. Lester is a friend of mine.'

Stacey looked at Lester with contempt. He did not like amateurs.

'Let me continue, and tell you how the obstacles can be overcome. First, the two store detectives. Supposing that a small fire bomb were planted in the Fur Department, at the other end of the third floor from Jewellery – that would certainly occupy one detective for a few minutes. Supposing that in the department that deals with ladies' hats, which is next to Furs, a woman shopper complained that she had been robbed – this would certainly involve the other store detective. Could you arrange this, Stace? These – assistants, shall I call them? – would be paid a straight fee. They would have to carry out their diversions at a precise time, which I have fixed as ten thirty in the morning.'

'Okay,' said Stacey. 'Consider it arranged.'

'Next, Davidson. He is an American, as I said, and Lester tells me that a happy event is expected in his family any day now. He has left Mrs Davidson behind in America, of course. Now, supposing that a call came through, apparently from an American hospital, for Mr Davidson. Supposing that the telephone in the Jewellery Department was out of order because the cord had been cut. Davidson would be called out of the department for the few minutes, no more, that we should need.'

'Who cuts the cord?' Stacey asked.

'That will be part of Lester's job.'

'And who makes the phone call?'

'Again, Stace, I hoped that you might be able to provide – '

'I can do that.' Stacey drained his whisky. 'But what do you do?'

Mr Payne's lips, never full, were compressed to a disapproving line. He answered the implied criticism only by inviting them to look at two maps – one the layout of the entire third floor, the other of the Jewellery Department itself. Stacey and Straight were impressed, as the uneducated always are, by such evidence of careful planning.

'The Jewellery Department is at one end of the third floor. It has only one exit – into the Carpet Department. There is a service lift which comes straight up into the Jewellery Department. You and I, Stace, will be in that. We shall stop it between floors with the Emergency Stop button. At exactly ten thirty-two we shall go up to the third floor. Lester will give us a sign. If everything has gone well, we proceed. If not, we call the job off. Now, what I propose ... '

He told them, they listened and they found it good. Even the ignorant, Mr Payne was glad to see, could recognise genius. He told Straight Line his role.

'We must have a car, Straight, and a driver. What he has to do is simple, but he must stay cool. So I thought of you.' Straight grinned.

'In Jessiter Street, just outside the side entrance to Orbin's, there is a parking space reserved for Orbin's customers. It is hardly ever full. But if it is full you can double park there for five minutes – cars often do that. I take it you can – acquire a car, shall I say? – for the purpose. You will face away from Oxford Street, and you will have no more than a few minutes' run to Lambie's house on Greenly Street. You will drop Stace and me, drive on a mile or two and leave the car. We shall give the stuff to Lambie. He will pay on the nail. Then we all split.'

From that point they went on to argue about the split. The argument was warm, but not really heated. They settled that Stacey would get 25 per cent of the total, Straight and Lester 12½ per cent each, and that half would go to the mastermind. Mr Payne agreed to provide out of his share the £150 that Stacey said would cover the three diversions.

The job was fixed six days ahead – for Tuesday of the following week.

Stacey had two faults which had prevented him from rising high in his profession. One was that he drank too much, the other that he was stupid. He made an effort to keep his drinking under control, knowing that when he drank he talked. So he did not even tell his wife about the job, although she was safe enough.

But he could not resist cheating about the money, which Payne had given to him in full.

The fire bomb was easy. Stacey got hold of a little man named Shrimp Bateson, and fixed it with him. There was no risk, and Shrimp thought himself well paid with twenty-five quid. The bomb itself cost only a fiver, from a friend who dealt in hardware. It was guaranteed to cause just a little fire, nothing serious.

For the telephone call Stacey used a Canadian who was

grubbing a living at a striptease club. It didn't seem to either of them that the job was worth more than a tenner, but the Canadian asked for twenty and got fifteen.

The woman was a different matter, for she had to be a bit of an actress, and she might be in for trouble since she actually had to cause a disturbance. Stacey hired an eighteen-stone Irish woman named Lucy O'Malley, who had once been a female wrestler, and had very little in the way of a record – nothing more than a couple of drunk and disorderlies. She refused to take anything less than £50, realising, as the others hadn't, that Stacey must have something big on.

The whole lot came to less than £100, so that there was cash to spare. Stacey paid them all half their money in advance, put the rest of the £100 aside and went on a roaring drunk for a couple of days, during which he somehow managed to keep his mouth buttoned and his nose clean.

When he reported on Monday night to Mr Payne he seemed to have everything fixed, including himself.

Straight Line was a reliable character, a young man who kept himself to himself. He pinched the car on Monday afternoon, took it along to the semi-legitimate garage run by his father-in-law and put new licence plates on it. There was no time for a respray job, but he roughed the car up a little so that the owner would be unlikely to recognise it if by an unlucky chance he should be passing outside Orbin's on Tuesday morning. During this whole operation, of course, Straight wore gloves.

He also reported to Mr Payne on Monday night.

Lester's name was not really Lester – it was Leonard. His mother and his friends in Balham, where he had been born and brought up, called him Lenny. He detested this, as he detested his surname and the pimples that, in spite of his assiduous efforts with ointment, appeared on his face every couple of months. There was nothing he could do about the name of Jones, because it was on his National Insurance card, but Lester for Leonard was a gesture towards emancipation.

Another gesture was made when he left home and mother for a one-room flat in Notting Hill Gate. A third gesture – and the most important one – was his friendship with Lucille, whom he had met in a jazz club called The Whizz Fizz.

Lucille called herself an actress, but the only evidence of it was that she occasionally sang in the club. Her voice was tuneless but loud. After she sang, Lester always bought her a drink, and the drink was always whisky.

'So what's new?' she said. 'Lester-boy what's new?'

'I sold a diamond necklace today. Two hundred and fifty pounds. Mr Marston was very pleased.' Mr Marston was the manager of the Jewellery Department.

'So Mr Marston was pleased. Big deal.' Lucille looked round restlessly, tapping her foot.

'He might give me a raise.'

'Another ten bob a week and a pension for your fallen arches.'

'Lucille, won't you – '

'No.' The peak of emancipation for Lester, a dream beyond which his thoughts really could not reach, was that one day Lucille would come to live with him. Far from that, she had not even slept with him yet. 'Look, Lester-boy I know what I want, and let's face it, you haven't got it.'

He was incautious enough to ask, 'What?'

'Money, moolah, the green folding stuff. Without it you're nothing, with it they can't hurt you.'

Lester was drinking whisky too, although he didn't really like it. Perhaps, but for the whisky, he would never have said, 'Supposing I had money?'

'What money? Where would you get it – draw it out of the Savings Bank?'

'I mean a lot of money.'

'Lester-boy I don't think in penny numbers. I'm talking about real money.'

The room was thick with smoke; the Whizz Fizz Kids were playing. Lester leaned back and said deliberately, 'Next week I'll have money – thousands of pounds.'

Lucille was about to laugh. Then she said, 'It's my turn to buy a drink, I'm feeling generous. Hey, Joe. Two more of the same.'

Later that night they lay on the bed in his one-room flat. She had let him make love to her, and he had told her everything.

'So the stuff's going to a man called Lambie in Greenly Street?'

Lester had never before drunk so much in one evening. Was it six whiskies or seven? He felt ill, and alarmed, 'Lucille, you won't say anything? I mean, I wasn't supposed to tell – '

'Relax. What do you take me for?' She touched his cheek with red-tipped nails. 'Besides, we shouldn't have secrets, should we?'

He watched her as she got off the bed and began to dress. 'Won't you stay? I mean, it would be all right with the landlady.'

'No can do, Lester-boy. See you at the club, though. Tomorrow night. Promise.'

'Promise.' When she had gone he turned over on to his side and groaned. He feared that he was going to be sick, and he was. Afterwards, he felt better.

Lucille went home to her flat in Earl's Court, which she shared with a man named Jim Baxter. He had been sent to Borstal for a robbery from a confectioner's which had involved considerable violence. Since then he had done two short stretches. He listened to what she had to say, then asked, 'What's this Lester like?'

'A creep.'

'Has he got the nerve to kid you, or do you think it's on the level, what he's told you?'

'He wouldn't kid me. He wants me to live with him when he's got the money. I said I might.'

Jim showed her what he thought of that idea. Then he said, 'Tuesday morning, eh. Until then, you play along with this creep. Any change in plans I want to know about it. You can do it, can't you, baby?'

She looked up at him. He had a scar on the left side of his face which she thought made him look immensely attractive. 'I can do it. And Jim?'

'Yes?'

'What about afterwards?'

'Afterwards, baby? Well, for spending money there's no place like London. Unless it's Paris.'

Lester Jones also reported on Monday night. Lucille was being very kind to him, so he no longer felt uneasy.

Mr Payne gave them all a final briefing and stressed that timing, in this as in every similar affair, was the vital element.

Mr Rossiter Payne rose on Tuesday morning at his usual time, just after eight o'clock. He bathed and shaved with care and precision, and ate his usual breakfast of one soft-boiled egg, two pieces of toast and one cup of unsugared coffee. When Miss Oliphant arrived he was already in the shop.

'My dear Miss Oliphant. Are you, as they say, ready to cope this morning?'

'Of course, Mr Payne. Do you have to go out?'

'I do. Something quite unexpected. An American collector named – but I mustn't tell his name even to you, he doesn't want it known – is in London, and he has asked me to see him. He wants to try to buy the manuscripts of – but there again I'm sworn to secrecy although if I weren't I should surprise you. I am calling on him, so I shall leave things in your care until – ' Mr Payne looked at his expensive watch – 'not later than midday. I shall certainly be back by then. In the meantime, Miss Oliphant, I entrust my ware to you.'

She giggled. 'I won't let anyone steal the stock, Mr Payne.'

Mr Payne went upstairs again to his flat, where, laid out on his bed, was a very different set of clothes from that which he normally wore. He emerged later from the little side entrance looking quite unlike the dapper, retired Guards officer known to Miss Oliphant.

His clothes were of the shabby nondescript-ready-to-wear kind that might be worn by a City clerk very much down on his luck – the sleeve and trouser cuffs distinctly frayed, the tie a piece of dirty string. Curling strands of rather disgustingly gingery hair strayed from beneath his stained grey trilby hat and his face was grey too – grey and much lined, the face of a man of sixty who has been defeated by life.

Mr Payne had bright blue eyes, but the man who came out of the side entrance had, thanks to contact lenses, brown ones. This man shuffled off down the alley with shoulders bent, carrying a rather dingy suitcase. He was quite unrecognisable as the upright Rossiter Payne.

Indeed, if there was a criticism to be made of him, it was that he looked almost too much the 'little man'. Long, long ago, Mr Payne had been an actor, and although his dramatic abilities were extremely limited, he had always loved and been extremely good at make-up.

He took with him a realistic-looking gun that, in fact, fired nothing more lethal than caps. He was a man who disliked violence, and thought it unnecessary.

After he left Mr Payne on Monday night, Stacey had been unable to resist having a few drinks. The alarm clock wakened him to a smell of frizzling bacon. His wife sensed that he had a job on, and she came into the bedroom as he was taking the Smith and Wesson out of the cupboard.

'Bill.' He turned round. 'Do you need that?'

'What do you think?'

'Don't take it.'

'Ah, don't be stupid.'

'Bill, please. I get frightened.'

Stacey put the gun into his hip pocket. 'Won't use it. Just makes me feel a bit more comfortable, see?'

He ate his breakfast with a good appetite and then telephoned Shrimp Bateson, Lucy O'Malley and the Canadian to make sure they were ready. They were. His wife watched him fearfully. Then he came to say goodbye.

'Bill, look after yourself.'

'Always do.' And he was gone.

Lucille had spent Monday night with Lester. This was much against her wish, but Jim had insisted on it, saying that he must know of any possible last-minute change.

Lester had no appetite at all. She watched with barely concealed contempt as he drank no more than half a cup of coffee and pushed aside his toast. When he got dressed his fingers were trembling so that he could hardly button his shirt.

'Today's the day, then.'

'Yes. I wish it was over.'

'Don't worry.'

He said eagerly, 'I'll see you in the club tonight.'

'Yes.'

'I shall have the money then, and we could go away together. Oh, no, of course not – I've got to stay on the job.'

'That's right,' she said, humouring him. As soon as he had gone, she rang Jim and reported that there were no last-minute changes.

Straight Line lived with his family. They knew he had a job on, but nobody talked about it. Only his mother stopped him at the door and said, 'Good luck, son,' and his father said, 'Keep your nose clean.'

Straight went to the garage and got out the Jag.

10:30.

Shrimp Bateson walked into the Fur Department with a brown-paper package under his arm. He strolled about pretending to look at furs, while trying to find a place to put down the little parcel. There were several shoppers, and he went unnoticed.

He stopped at the point where Furs led to the stairs, moved into a window embrasure, took the little metal cylinder out of its brown-paper wrapping, pressed the switch which started the mechanism and walked rapidly away.

He had almost reached the door when he was tapped on the shoulder. He turned. A clerk was standing with the brown paper in his hand.

'Excuse me, sir, I think you've dropped something. I found this paper – '

'No, no,' Shrimp said. 'It's not mine.'

There was no time to waste in arguing. Shrimp turned and half walked, half ran, through the doors and to the staircase. The clerk followed him. People were coming up the stairs, and Shrimp, in a desperate attempt to avoid them, slipped and fell, bruising his shoulder.

The clerk was standing hesitantly at the top of the stairs when he heard the *whoosh* of sound and, turning, saw flames. He ran down the stairs then, took Shrimp firmly by the arm and said, 'I think you'd better come back with me, sir.'

The bomb had gone off on schedule, setting fire to the window curtains and to one end of a store counter. A few women were screaming, and other clerks were busy saving the furs. Flack, one of the store detectives, arrived on the spot quickly, and organised the use of the fire extinguishers. They got the fire completely under control in three minutes.

The clerk, full of zeal, brought Shrimp along to Flack. 'Here's the man who did it.'

Flack looked at him. 'Firebug, eh?'

'Let me go. I had nothing to do with it.'

'Let's talk to the manager, shall we?' Flack said, and led Shrimp away.

The time was now 10:39.

Lucy O'Malley looked at herself in the glass, and at the skimpy hat perched on her enormous head. Her fake-crocodile handbag, of a size to match her person, had been put down on a chair near by.

'What do you feel, madam?' the young saleswoman asked, ready to take her cue from the customer's reaction.

'Terrible.'

'Perhaps it isn't really you.'

'It looks bloody awful,' Lucy said. She enjoyed swearing, and saw no reason why she should restrain herself

The salesgirl laughed perfunctorily and dutifully, and moved over again towards the hats. She indicated a black hat with a wide brim. 'Perhaps something more like this?'

Lucy looked at her watch. 10:31. It was time. She went across to her handbag, opened it and screamed.

'Is something the matter, madam?'

'I've been robbed!'

'Oh, really, I don't think that can have happened.'

Lucy had a sergeant-major's voice, and she used it. 'Don't tell me what can and can't have happened, young woman.

My money was in here, and now it's gone. Somebody's taken it.'

The salesgirl, easily intimidated, blushed. The department supervisor, elegant, eagle-nosed, blue-rinsed, moved across like an arrow and asked politely if she could help.

'My money's been stolen,' Lucy shouted. 'I put my bag down for a minute, twenty pounds in it, and now it's gone. That's the class of people they get in Orbin's.' She addressed this last sentence to another shopper, who moved away hurriedly.

'Let's look, shall we, just to make sure.' Blue Rinse took hold of the handbag, Lucy took hold of it too and somehow the bag's contents spilled onto the carpet.

'You stupid fool,' Lucy roared.

'I'm sorry, madam,' Blue Rinse said icily. She picked up handkerchief, lipstick, powder compact, tissues. Certainly there was no money in the bag. 'You're sure the money was in the bag?'

'Of course I'm sure. It was in my purse. I had it five minutes ago. Someone here has stolen it.'

'Not so loud, please, madam.'

'I shall speak as loudly as I like. Where's your store detective, or haven't you got one?'

Sidley, the other detective on the third floor, was pushing through the little crowd that had collected. 'What seems to be the matter?'

'This lady says twenty pounds has been stolen from her handbag.' Blue Rinse just managed to refrain from emphasising the word 'lady'.

'I'm very sorry. Shall we talk about it in the office?'

'I don't budge until I get my money back.' Lucy was carrying an umbrella, and she waved it threateningly. However, she allowed herself to be led along to the office. There the handbag was examined again and the salesgirl, now tearful, was interrogated. There also Lucy, having surreptitiously glanced at the time, put a hand into the capacious pocket of her coat, and discovered the purse. There was twenty pounds in it, just as she had said.

She apologised, although the apology went much against the grain for her, declined the suggestion that she should return to the hat counter and left the store with the consciousness of a job well done.

'Well, Sidley, I shouldn't like to tangle with her on a dark night.'

The time was now 10:40.

The clock in the Jewellery Department stood at exactly 10:33 when a girl came running in, out of breath, and said to the manager, 'Oh, Mr Marston, there's a telephone call for Mr Davidson. It's from America.'

Marston was large, and inclined to be pompous. 'Put it through here, then.'

'I can't. There's something wrong with the line in this department – it seems to be dead.'

Davidson had heard his name mentioned, and came over to them quickly. He was a crew-cut American, tough and lean. 'It'll be about my wife, she's expecting a baby. Where's the call?'

'We've got it in Administration, one floor up.'

'Come on, then.' Davidson started off at what was almost

a run, and the girl trotted after him. Marston stared at both of them disapprovingly. He became aware that one of his clerks, Lester Jones, was looking rather odd.

'Is anything the matter, Jones? Do you feel unwell?'

Lester said that he was all right. The act of cutting the telephone cord had filled him with terror, but with the departure of Davidson he really did feel better. He thought of the money – and of Lucille.

Lucille was just saying goodbye to Jim Baxter and his friend Eddie Grain. They were equipped with an arsenal of weapons, including flick knives, bicycle chains and brass knuckles. They did not, however, carry revolvers.

'You'll be careful,' Lucille said to Jim.

'Don't worry. This is going to be like taking candy from a baby, isn't it, Eddie?'

'S'right,' Eddie said. He had a limited vocabulary, and an almost perpetual smile. He was a terror with a knife.

The Canadian made the call from the striptease club. He had a girl with him. He had told her that it would be a big giggle. When he heard Davidson's voice – the time was just after ten thirty-four – he said, 'Is that Mr Davidson?'

'Yes.'

'This is the James Long Foster Hospital in Chicago, Mr Davidson, Maternity floor.'

'Yes?'

'Will you speak up, please. I can't hear you very well.'

'Have you got some news of my wife?' Davidson said loudly. He was in a small booth next to the store switchboard. There was no reply. 'Hello? Are you there?'

The Canadian put one hand over the receiver, and ran the other up the girl's bare thigh. 'Let him stew a little.' The girl laughed. They could hear Davidson asking if they were still on the line. Then the Canadian spoke again.

'Hello, hello, Mr Davidson. We seem to have a bad connection.'

'I can hear you clearly. What news is there?'

'No need to worry, Mr Davidson. Your wife is fine.'

'Has she had the baby?'

The Canadian chuckled. 'Now, don't be impatient. That's not the kind of thing you can hurry, you know.'

'What have you got to tell me then? Why are you calling?'

The Canadian put his hand over the receiver again, said to the girl, 'You say something.'

'What shall I say?'

'Doesn't matter – that we've got the wires crossed or something.'

The girl leaned over, picked up the telephone. 'This is the operator. Who are you calling?'

In the telephone booth sweat was running off Davidson. He hammered with his fist on the wall of the booth. 'Damn you, get off the line! Put me back to the Maternity floor.'

'This is the operator. Who do you want, please?'

Davidson checked himself suddenly. The girl had a Cockney voice. 'Who are you? What's your game?'

The girl handed the telephone back to the Canadian, looking frightened. 'He's on to me.'

'Hell.' The Canadian picked up the receiver again, but the girl had left it uncovered, and Davidson had heard the girl's words. He dropped the telephone, pushed open the door of the booth and raced for the stairs. As he ran he loosened the revolver in his hip pocket.

The time was now 10:41.

Straight Line brought the Jaguar smoothly to a stop in the space reserved for Orbin's customers, and looked at his watch. It was 10:32.

Nobody questioned him, nobody so much as gave him a glance. Beautiful, he thought, a nice smooth job, really couldn't be simpler. Then his hands tightened on the steering wheel.

He saw in the rear-view mirror, standing just a few yards behind him, a policeman. Three men were evidently asking the policeman for directions, and the copper was consulting a London place map.

Well, Straight thought, he can't see anything of me except my back, and in a couple of minutes he'll be gone. There was still plenty of time. Payne and Stacey weren't due out of the building until 10:39 or 10:40. Yes, plenty of time.

But there was a hollow feeling in Straight's stomach as he watched the policeman in his mirror.

Some minutes earlier, at 10:24, Payne and Stacey had met at the service elevator beside the Grocery Department on the ground floor. They had met this early because of the possibility that the elevator might be in use when they needed it, although from Lester's observation it was used mostly in the early morning and late afternoon.

They did not need the elevator until 10:30, and they would be very unlucky if it was permanently in use at that time. If they were that unlucky – well, Mr Payne had said with the pseudo-philosophy of the born gambler, they would have to call the job off. But even as he said this he knew that it was not true, and that having gone so far he would not turn back.

The two men did not speak to each other, but advanced steadily toward the elevator by way of inspecting chow mein, hymettus honey and real turtle soup. The Grocery Department was full of shoppers, and the two men were quite unnoticed. Mr Payne reached the elevator first and pressed the button. They were in luck. The door opened.

Within seconds they were both inside. Still neither man spoke. Mr Payne pressed the button which said 3, and then, when they had passed the second floor, the button that said Emergency Stop. Jarringly the elevator came to a stop. It was now immobilised, so far as a call from outside was concerned. It could be put back into motion only by calling in engineers who would free the Emergency Stop mechanism – or, of course, by operating the elevator from inside.

Stacey shivered a little. The elevator was designed for freight, and therefore roomy enough to hold twenty passengers; but Stacey had a slight tendency to claustrophobia, which was increased by the thought that they were poised between floors. He said, 'I suppose that bloody thing will work when you press the button?'

'Don't worry, my friend. Have faith in me.' Mr Payne opened the dingy suitcase, revealing as he did so that he was now wearing rubber gloves. In the suitcase were two long red cloaks, two fuzzy white wigs, two thick white beards, two pairs of outsize horn-rimmed spectacles, two red noses and two hats with large tassels. 'This may not be a perfect fit for you, but I don't think you can deny that it's a perfect disguise.'

They put on the clothes, Mr Payne with the pleasure he always felt in dressing up, Stacey with a certain reluctance. The idea was clever, all right, he had to admit that, and when he looked in the elevator's small mirror and saw a Santa Claus looking back at him, he was pleased to find himself totally unrecognisable. Deliberately he took the Smith and Wesson out of his jacket and put it into the pocket of the red cloak.

'You understand, Stace, there is no question of using that weapon.'

'Unless I have to.'

'There is no question,' Mr Payne repeated firmly. 'Violence is never necessary. It is a confession that one lacks intelligence.'

'We got to point it at them, haven't we? Show we mean business.'

Mr Payne acknowledged that painful necessity by a downward twitch of his mouth, undiscernible beneath the false beard.

'Isn't it time, yet?'

Mr Payne looked at his watch. 'It is now ten twenty-nine. We go – over the top, you might call it – at ten thirty-two precisely. Compose yourself to wait, Stace.'

Stacey grunted. He could not help admiring his companion, who stood peering into the small glass, adjusting his beard and moustache, and settling his cloak more comfortably. When at last Mr Payne nodded, and said, 'Here we go,' and pressed the button marked 3, resentment was added to admiration. He's all right now, but wait till we get to the action, Stacey thought. His gloved hand on the Smith and Wesson reassured him of strength and efficiency.

The elevator shuddered, moved upwards, stopped. The door opened. Mr Payne placed his suitcase in the open elevator door so that it would stay open and keep the elevator at the third floor. Then they stepped out.

To Lester the time that passed after Davidson's departure and before the elevator door opened was complete and absolute torture.

The whole thing had seemed so easy when Mr Payne had outlined it to them. 'It is simply a matter of perfect timing,' he had said. 'If everybody plays his part properly, Stace and I will be back in the lift within five minutes. Planning is the essence of this, as of every scientific operation. Nobody will be hurt, and nobody will suffer financially except – ' and here he had looked at Lester with a twinkle in his frosty eyes – 'except the insurance company. And I don't think the most tender-hearted of us will worry too much about the insurance company.'

That was all very well, and Lester had done what he was supposed to do, but he hadn't really been able to believe that the rest of it would happen. He had been terrified, but with the terror was mixed a sense of unreality.

He still couldn't believe, even when Davidson went to the telephone upstairs, that the plan would go through without a hitch. He was showing some costume jewellery to a thin old woman who kept roping necklaces around her scrawny neck, and while he did so he kept looking at the elevator, above which was the department clock. The hands moved slowly, after Davidson left, from 10:31 to 10:32.

They're not coming, Lester thought. It's all off. A flood of relief, touched with regret but with relief predominating, went through him. Then the elevator door opened, and the two Santa Clauses stepped out. Lester started convulsively.

'Young man,' the thin woman said severely, 'it doesn't seem to me that I have your undivided attention. Haven't you anything in blue and amber?'

It had been arranged that Lester would nod to signify that Davidson had left the department, or shake his head if anything had gone wrong. He nodded now as though he had St Vitus's Dance.

The thin woman looked at him, astonished, 'Young man, is anything the matter?'

'Blue and amber,' Lester said wildly, 'amber and blue.' He pulled out a box from under the counter and began to look through it. His hands were shaking.

Mr Payne had been right in his assumption that no surprise would be occasioned by the appearance of two Santa Clauses in any department at this time of year. This, he liked to think, was his own characteristic touch – the touch of, not to be unduly modest about it, creative genius. There were a dozen people in the Jewellery Department, half of them looking at the Russian Royal Family Jewels, which had proved less of an attraction than Sir Henry Orbin had hoped. Three of the others were wandering about in the idle way of people who are not really intending to buy anything, and the other three were at the counters, where they were being attended to by Lester, a salesgirl whose name was Miss Glenny and by Marston himself.

The appearance of the Santa Clauses aroused only the feeling of pleasure experienced by most people at sight of these slightly artificial figures of jollity. Even Marston barely glanced at them. There were half a dozen Santa Clauses in the store during the weeks before Christmas, and he assumed that these two were on their way to the Toy Department, which was also on the third floor, or to the Robin Hood in Sherwood Forest tableau, which was this year's display for children.

The Santa Clauses walked across the floor together as though they were in fact going into Carpets, and then on to the Toy Department, but after passing Lester they diverged. Mr Payne went to the archway that led from Jewellery to Carpets, and Stacey abruptly turned behind Lester towards the Manager's Office.

Marston, trying to sell an emerald brooch to an American who was not at all sure his wife would like it, looked up in surprise. He had a natural reluctance to make a fuss in public, and also to leave his customer; but when he saw Stacey with a hand actually on the door of his own small but sacred office he said to the American, 'Excuse me a moment, sir,' and said to Miss Glenny, 'Look after this gentleman, please' – by which he meant that the American should not be allowed to walk out with the emerald brooch – and called out, although not so loudly that the call could be thought of as anything so vulgar as a shout, 'Just a moment, please. What are you doing there? What do you want?'

Stacey ignored him. In doing so he was carrying out Mr

Payne's specific instructions. At some point it was inevitable that the people in the department would realise that a theft was taking place, but the longer they could be kept from realising it, Mr Payne had said, the better. Stacey's own inclination would have been to pull out his revolver at once and terrorise anybody likely to make trouble; but he did as he was told.

The Manager's Office was not much more than a cubbyhole, with papers neatly arranged on a desk; behind the desk, half a dozen keys were hanging on the wall. The showcase key, Lester had said, was the second from the left, but for the sake of appearances Stacey took all the keys. He had just turned to go when Marston opened the door and saw the keys in Stacey's hand.

The manager was not lacking in courage. He understood at once what was happening and, without speaking, tried to grapple with the intruder. Stacey drew the Smith and Wesson from his pocket and struck Marston hard with it on the forehead. The manager dropped to the ground. A trickle of blood came from his head. The office door was open, and there was no point in making any further attempt at deception. Stacey swung the revolver around and rasped, 'Just keep quiet, and nobody else will get hurt.'

Mr Payne produced his cap pistol and said, in a voice as unlike his usual cultured tones as possible, 'Stay where you are. Don't move. We shall be gone in five minutes.'

Somebody said, 'Well, I'm damned.' But no one moved. Marston lay on the floor, groaning. Stacey went to the showcase, pretended to fumble with another key, then inserted the right one. The case opened at once. The jewels lay naked and unprotected. He dropped the other keys on the floor, stretched in his gloved hands, picked up the royal jewels and stuffed them into his pocket.

It's going to work, Lester thought unbelievingly, it's going to work. He watched, fascinated, as the cascade of shining stuff vanished into Stacey's pocket. Then he became aware that the thin woman was pressing something into his hand. Looking down, he saw with horror that it was a large, brand-new clasp knife, with the dangerous-looking blade open.

'Bought it for my nephew,' the thin woman whispered. 'As he passes you, go for him.'

It had been arranged that if Lester's behaviour should arouse the least suspicion he should make a pretend attack on Stacey, who would give him a punch just severe enough to knock him down. Everything had gone so well, however, that this had not been necessary, but now it seemed to Lester that he had no choice.

As the two Santa Clauses backed across the room toward the service elevator, covering the people at the counters with their revolvers, one real and the other a toy, Lester launched himself feebly at Stacey, with the clasp knife demonstratively raised. At the same time Marston, on the other side of Stacey and a little behind him, rose to his feet and staggered in the direction of the elevator.

Stacey's contempt for Lester increased with the sight of the knife, which he regarded as an unnecessary bit of bravado. He shifted the revolver to his left hand, and with his right punched Lester hard in the stomach. The blow doubled Lester up. He dropped the knife and collapsed to the floor, writhing in quite genuine pain.

The delivery of the blow delayed Stacey so that Marston was almost up to him. Mr Payne, retreating rapidly to the elevator, shouted a warning, but the manager was on Stacey, clawing at his robes. He did not succeed in pulling off the red cloak, but his other hand came away with the wig, revealing Stacey's own cropped brown hair. Stacey snatched back the wig, broke away and fired the revolver with his left hand.

Perhaps he could hardly have said himself whether he intended to hit Marston or simply to stop him. The bullet missed the manager and hit Lester, who was rising on one knee. Lester dropped again. Miss Glenny screamed, another woman cried out and Marston halted.

Mr Payne and Stacey were almost at the elevator when Davidson came charging in through the Carpet Department entrance. The American drew the revolver from his pocket and shot, all in one swift movement. Stacey fired back wildly. Then the two Santa Clauses were in the service elevator, and the door closed on them.

Davidson took one look at the empty showcase, and shouted to Marston, 'Is there an emergency alarm that rings downstairs?'

The manager shook his head. 'And my telephone's not working.'

'They've cut the line.' Davidson raced back through the Carpet Department to the passenger elevators.

Marston went over to where Lester was lying, with half a dozen people round him, including the thin woman. 'We must get a doctor.'

The American he had been serving said, 'I am a doctor.' He was bending over Lester, whose eyes were wide open.

'How is he?'

The American lowered his voice. 'He got it in the abdomen.'

Lester seemed to be trying to raise himself up. The thin woman helped him. He sat up, looked around, and said, 'Lucille.' Then blood suddenly rushed out of his mouth, and he sank back.

The doctor bent over again, then looked up. 'I'm very sorry. He's dead.'

The thin woman gave Lester a more generous obituary than he deserved. 'He wasn't a very good clerk, but he was a brave young man.'

Straight Line, outside in the stolen Jag, waited for the policeman to move. But not a bit of it. The three men with the policeman were pointing to a particular spot on the map, and the copper was laughing; they were having some sort of stupid joke together. What the hell, Straight thought. Hasn't the bleeder got any work to do, doesn't he know he's not supposed to be hanging about?

Straight looked at his watch. 10:34, coming up to 10:35 – and now, as the three men finally moved away, what should happen but that a teenage girl should come up, and the copper was bending over towards her with a look of holiday good-will.

It's no good, Straight thought, I shall land them right in his lap if I stay here. He pulled away from the parking space, looked again at his watch. He was obsessed by the need to get out of the policeman's sight.

Once round the block, he thought, just once round can't

take more than a minute, and I've got more than two minutes to spare. Then if the copper's still here I'll stay a few yards away from him with my engine running.

He moved down Jessiter Street and a moment after Straight had gone, the policeman, who had never even glanced at him, moved away too.

By Mr Payne's plan they should have taken off their Santa Claus costumes in the service elevator and walked out at the bottom as the same respectable, anonymous citizens who had gone in; but as soon as they were inside the elevator Stacey said, 'He hit me.' A stain showed on the scarlet right arm of his robe.

Mr Payne pressed the button to take them down. He was proud that, in this emergency, his thoughts came with clarity and logic. He spoke them aloud.

'No time to take these off. Anyway, they're just as good a disguise in the street. Straight will be waiting. We step out and into the car, take them off there. Davidson shouldn't have been back in that department for another two minutes.

'I gotta get to a doctor.'

'We'll go to Lambie's first. He'll fix it.' The elevator whirred downward. Almost timidly, Mr Payne broached the subject that worried him most. 'What happened to Lester?'

'He caught one.' Stacey was pale.

The elevator stopped. Mr Payne adjusted the wig on Stacey's head. 'They can't possibly be waiting for us, there hasn't been time. We just walk out. Not too fast, remember. Casually, normally.'

The elevator door opened and they walked the fifty

feet to the Jessiter Street exit. They were delayed only by a small boy who rushed up to Mr Payne, clung to his legs and shouted that he wanted his Christmas present. Mr Payne gently disengaged him, whispered to his mother, 'Our tea break. Back later,' and moved on.

Now they were outside in the street. But there was no sign of Straight or the Jaguar.

Stacey began to curse. They crossed the road from Orbin's, stood outside Danny's Shoe Parlour for a period that seemed to both of them endless but was, in fact, only thirty seconds. People looked at them curiously – two Santa Clauses wearing false noses – but they did not arouse great attention. They were oddities, yes, but oddities were in keeping with the time of year and Oxford Street's festive decorations.

'We've got to get away,' Stacey said. 'We're sitting ducks.'

'Don't be a fool. We wouldn't get a hundred yards.'

'Planning,' Stacey said bitterly. 'Fine bloody planning. If you ask me – '

'Here he is.'

The Jag drew up beside them, and in a moment they were in and down Jessiter Street, away from Orbin's. Davidson was on the spot less than a minute later, but by the time he had found passers-by who had seen the two Santa Clauses get into the car, they were half a mile away.

Straight Line began to explain what had happened, Stacey swore at him and Mr Payne cut them both short.

'No time for that. Get these clothes off, talk later.'

'You got the rocks?'

'Yes, but Stace has been bit. By the American detective. I don't think it's bad, though.'

'Whatsisname, Lester, he OK?'

'There was trouble. Stace caught him with a bullet.'

Straight said nothing more. He was not one to complain about something that couldn't be helped. His feelings showed only in the controlled savagery with which he manoeuvred the Jag.

While Straight drove, Mr Payne was taking off his own Santa Claus outfit and helping Stacey off with his. He stuffed them, with the wigs and beards and noses, back into the suitcase. Stacey winced as the robe came over his right arm, and Mr Payne gave him a handkerchief to hold over it. At the same time he suggested that Stacey hand over the jewels, since Mr Payne would be doing the negotiating with the fence. It was a mark of the trust that both men still reposed in Mr Payne that Stacey handed them over without a word, and that Straight did not object or even comment. They turned into the quiet Georgian terrace where Lambie lived. 'Number Fifteen, right-hand side,' Mr Payne said.

Jim Baxter and Eddie Grain had been hanging about in the street for several minutes. Lucille had learned from Lester what car Straight was driving. They recognised the Jag immediately, and strolled towards it. They had just reached the car when it came to a stop in front of Lambie's house. Stacey and Mr Payne got out. Jim and Eddie were not, after all, too experienced. They made an elementary mistake in not waiting until Straight had driven away. Jim had his flick knife out and was pointing it at Mr Payne's stomach.

'Come on now, Dad, give us the stuff and you won't get hurt,' he said.

On the other side of the car Eddie Grain, less subtle, swung at Stacey with a shortened length of bicycle chain. Stacey, hit round the head, went down, and Eddie was on top of him, kicking, punching, searching.

Mr Payne hated violence, but he was capable of defending himself. He stepped aside, kicked upwards and knocked the knife flying from Jim's hand. Then he rang the doorbell of Lambie's house. At the same time Straight got out of the car and felled Eddie Grain with a vicious rabbit punch.

During the next few minutes several things happened simultaneously. At the end of the road a police whistle was blown, loudly and insistently, by an old lady who had seen what was going on.

Lambie, who also saw what was going on and wanted no part of it, told his manservant on no account to answer the doorbell or open the door.

Stacey, kicked and beaten by Eddie Grain, drew his revolver and fired four shots. One of them struck Eddie in the chest, and another hit Jim Baxter in the leg. Eddie scuttled down the street holding his chest, turned the corner and ran slap into the arms of two policemen hurrying to the scene.

Straight, who did not care for shooting, got back into the Jag and drove away. He abandoned the Jag as soon as he could, and went home.

When the police arrived, with a bleating Eddie in tow, they found Stacey and Jim Baxter on the ground, and several neighbours only too ready to tell confusing stories about the great gang fight that had just taken place. They interrogated Lambie, of course, but he had not seen or heard anything at all.

And Mr Payne? With a general melee taking place, and Lambie clearly not intending to answer his doorbell, he had walked away down the road. When he turned the corner he found a cab, which he took to within a couple of hundred yards of his shop. Then, an anonymous man carrying a shabby suitcase, he went in through the little side entrance.

Things had gone badly, he reflected as he again became Mr Rossiter Payne the antiquarian bookseller, mistakes had been made. But happily they were not his mistakes. The jewels would be hot, no doubt; they would have to be kept for a while, but all was not lost.

Stace and Straight were professionals – they would never talk. And although Mr Payne did not, of course, know that Lester was dead, he realised that the young man would be able to pose as a wounded hero and was not likely to be subjected to severe questioning.

So Mr Payne was whistling 'There's a Silver Lining' as he went down to greet Miss Oliphant.

'Oh, Mr Payne,' she trilled. 'You're back before you said. It's not half-past eleven.'

Could that be true? Yes, it was.

'Did the American collector – I mean, will you be able to sell him the manuscripts?'

'I hope so. Negotiations are proceeding, Miss Oliphant. They may take some time, but I hope they will reach a successful conclusion.'

The time passed uneventfully until 2:30 in the afternoon, when Miss Oliphant entered his little private office. 'Mr Payne, there are two gentlemen to see you. They won't say what it's about, but they look – well, rather funny.'

As soon as Mr Payne saw them, and even before they produced their warrant cards, he knew that there was nothing funny about them. He took them up to the flat and tried to talk his way out of it, but he knew it was no use. They hadn't yet got search warrants, the Inspector said, but they would be taking Payne along anyway. It would save them some trouble if he would care to show them –

Mr Payne showed them. He gave them the jewels and the Santa Claus disguises. Then he sighed at the weakness of subordinates. 'Somebody squealed, I suppose.'

'Oh, no. I'm afraid the truth is you were a bit careless.'

'*I* was careless.' Mr Payne was genuinely scandalised.

'Yes. You were recognised.'

'Impossible!'

'Not at all. When you left Orbin's and got out into the street, there was a bit of a mix-up so that you had to wait. Isn't that right?'

'Yes, but I was completely disguised.'

'Danny the shoeshine man knows you by name, doesn't he?'

'Yes, but he couldn't possibly have seen me.'

'He didn't need to. Danny can't see any faces from his basement, as you know, but he did see something, and he came to tell us about it. He saw two pairs of legs, and the bottoms of some sort of red robes. And he saw the shoes. He recognised one pair of shoes, Mr Payne. Not those you're wearing now, but that pair on the floor over there.'

Mr Payne looked across the room at the black shoes — shoes so perfectly appropriate to the role of shabby little clerk that he had been playing, and at the decisive, fatally recognisable sharp cut made by the bicycle mudguard in the black leather.

Nebuchadnezzar

Dorothy L. Sayers

You have played 'Nebuchadnezzar', of course – unless you are so ingenuous as never to have heard of any game but Yo-yo, or whatever the latest fad may be. 'Nebuchadnezzar' is so old-fashioned that only the sophisticated play it. It came back with charades, of which, of course, it is only a variation. It is called 'Nebuchadnezzar', I suppose, because you could not easily find a more impossible name with which to play it.

You choose a name – and unless your audience is very patient, it had better be a short one – of some well-known character. Say, Job. Then you act in dumb show a character beginning with J, then one beginning with O, then one beginning with B. Then you act Job, and the spectators guess that Job is what you mean, and applaud kindly. That is all. Light-hearted people, with imagination, can get a lot of fun out of it.

Bob Lester was having a birthday party – his mother and sister and about twenty intimate friends squashed into the little flat at Hammersmith. Everybody was either a writer or a painter or an actor of sorts, or did something or the other quite entertaining for a living, and they were fairly well accustomed to amusing themselves with sing-songs and games. They could fool wittily and behave like children, and get merry on invisible quantities of claretcup, and they were all rather clever and all knew each other extremely well. Cyril Markham felt slightly out of it, though they were all exceedingly nice to him and tried to cheer him up. It was nearly six months since Jane had died, and though they all sympathised terribly with him for her loss (they had all loved Jane), he felt that he and they were, and ever would be, strangers and aliens to one another. Dear Jane. They had found it hard to forgive him for marrying her and taking her away to Cornwall. It was terrible that she should have died – only two years later – of gastroenteritis. Jane would have entered into all their jokes. She would have played absurd games with them and given an exquisite personal grace to the absurdest. Markham could never do that. He felt stiff, awkward, cruelly self-conscious. When Bob suggested 'Nebuchadnez-zar', he courteously asked Markham to make one of his team of actors. Too kind, too kind. Markham said he preferred to look on, and Bob, sighing with relief, went on to pick up a side of trusted veterans.

The two front rooms of the flat had been thrown into one by the opening of the folding doors. Though it was November, the night was strangely close, and one of the three tall balconied windows overlooking the river had been thrown open. Across the smoke-filled room and over the heads of the guests, Markham could see the lights of the Surrey side dance in the river like tall Japanese lanterns. The smaller of the two rooms formed a stage for the players, and across the dividing doorway a pair of thick purple curtains had been hung. Outside, in the passage, the players scuffled backwards and forwards amid laughter. Waiting for the game to begin, Markham stared at the curtains. They were familiar. They were surely the curtains from his own Cornish cottage. Jane had hung them across the living room to screen off the dining part from the lounge part. How odd that Bob should have got them here. No, it wasn't. Bob had given Jane her curtains for a wedding present, and this must be another pair. They were old ones, he knew. Damask of that quality wasn't made today.

Bob drew back the curtains, thrust out a dishevelled head, announced 'The Nebuchadnezzar has four letters' and disappeared again. In the distance was heard a vigorous bumping, and a voice called out, 'There's a clothes line in the kitchen!' Somebody standing near the door of the room switched off the lights, and the damask curtains were drawn aside for the acting of the first letter.

A Japanese screen at the back of the stage, above which appeared the head of Lavinia Forbes, elegantly attired in a silk scarf, bound round the forehead with a cricket belt, caused Mrs Lester, always precipitate, to exclaim, 'Romeo and Juliet – balcony scene!' Everybody said 'Hush,' and the supposed Juliet, producing from behind the screen a mirror and lipstick, proceeded to make up her face in a very lavish manner. In the middle of this, her attention appeared to be distracted by something in the distance. She leaned over the screen and pointed eagerly in the direction of the landing, whence, indeed, some remarkable noises were proceeding. To her, amid frenzied applause, entered, on hands and knees, the twins, Peter and Paul Barnaby, got up regardless of expense in fur coats worn with the hair outside, and champing furiously upon the clothes line. Attached to them by stout luggage straps was a basket chair, which, after ominous hesitation and creaking between the doorposts was propelled vigorously into the room by unseen hands, so that the charioteer – very gorgeous in scarlet dressing-gown, striped sash and military sabre, with a large gravy strainer inverted upon his head – was nearly shot on to the backs of his steeds, and was heard to mutter an indignant 'Steady on!' through his forest of crêpe beard. The lady, from behind the screen, appeared to harangue the driver, who replied with a vulgar and regrettable gesture. A further brief exchange of pantomime led to the appearance of two stout parties in bath robes and turbans, who proceeded to hoist the lady bodily over the screen. Somebody said, 'Look out!', the screen rocked and was hastily held up by one of the horses, and the victim was deposited on the floor with a thud, and promptly died with a considerable amount of twitching and gasping. The charioteer cracked his umbrella across the backs of his horses and was drawn round the room and off again in a masterly manner. A loud barking from the wings heralded the arrival of three savage doormats, who, after snuffling a good deal over the corpse, started to devour it in large gulps as the curtain fell.

This spirited presentation was loudly cheered, and offered little difficulty to the spectators.

'Jezebel, of course,' said Tony Withers.

'Or Jehu,' said Miss Holroyd.

'I do hope Lavvie wasn't hurt,' said Mrs Lester. 'She came down an awful bump.'

'Well, the first letter's J, anyhow,' said Patricia Martin. 'I liked the furious driving.'

'Bob looked simply marvellous,' added Bice Taylor, who was sitting just behind Mrs Lester. Then, turning to Markham:

'But one does so miss darling Jane. She loved acting and dressing up, didn't she? She was the gayest wee bit of a thing.'

Markham nodded. Yes, Jane had always been an actress. And her gaiety had been somehow proof against the solitude of their cottage and his own morose temper. She always would sing as she went about the house, and it had got so terribly on his nerves that he had snarled at her. He had always wondered what she found to sing about. Until, of course, he had found those letters, and then he had known.

He wished he had not come to this party. He was out of place here, and Tom Deering knew it and was sneering at him. He could see Tom's dark, sardonic face in the far corner against the door. He must be remembering things too, the sleek devil. Well he, Markham, had put a spoke in Deering's wheel anyhow, that was one comfort.

In spite of the open window, the room was stifling. What did they need with that enormous fire? The blood was pumping violently through his brain – he felt as though the top of his head would lift off. There were far too many people for the place. And they made so much noise. Something fearfully elaborate must be in preparation, to judge by the long wait and the running of feet on the landing. This was a tedious game.

The lights clicked off once more, and a voice announced 'Second letter', as the curtains drew apart.

The apparition of Betty Sander in an exiguous pair of pale pink cami-bockers, with her hair down her back, embracing the deeply embarrassed George P. Brewster in a tight-fitting gent's union suit, was hailed with happy laughter.

'The bedroom scene!' exclaimed Mrs Lester, prematurely as usual. After an affecting exchange of endearments, the couple separated, George retiring to the far side of the piano to dig industriously with the coal scoop, while Betty seated herself on the sofa and combed her hair with her fingers. Presently there advanced through the door the crimson face of Peter Barnaby, worming along at ground-level, with energetically working tongue. Behind it trailed an endless length of green tablecloth, whose slow, humping progress proclaimed the presence within it of yet another human engine – probably the second Barnaby twin. This procession advanced to the sofa and rubbed itself against Betty's leg – then reared itself up rather awkwardly in its mufflings and jerked its head at the aspidistra on the occasional table. Betty registered horror and refusal, but presently yielded and took from amid the leaves of the aspidistra a large apple, which she proceeded to eat with expressions of enjoyment, while the combined Barnabys retired behind the sofa. At this moment, George, wiping the honest sweat from his brow, returned from his labours, with the coal scoop over his shoulder. On seeing what Betty was about, he dropped the scoop and flung his arms to heaven. After some solicitation, however, he accepted his share of the feast, carefully polishing the apple first on his union suit. After this, he appeared to be suddenly struck by the indelicacy of the union suit and, moreover, proceeded to point the finger of scorn and reprimand at the cami-bockers. Betty, dissolved in tears, pushed to the aspidistra, tore off two large leaves ('Oh, the poor plant!' cried Mrs Lester) and attached them severally, with string, about the waists of George and herself. Then, from behind the Japanese screen appeared the awful presence of Bob, in the scarlet dressing-gown and a bright blue tablecloth, and wearing a large saucepan lid tied to the back of his head. An immense beard of cotton-wool added majesty to his countenance. The delinquents fell flat on their faces, and the curtains were flung to amid rejoicings.

'Now, was that Adam and Eve?' demanded Miss Holroyd.

'I think it was Eve,' said somebody. 'Then the whole word might be Jehu.'

'But we've had Jehu.'

'No, we haven't, that was Jezebel.'

'But they can't be giving us Jehu and Jezebel again.'

'JE, JA, JE, JA ... '

The lights were on again now. Queer, how white and unnatural all their faces looked. Like masks. Markham's fingers pulled at his collar. Jezebel, Adam – Wanton woman, deluded man. J, A, Jane. So long as the whoredoms of thy mother Jezebel and her witchcrafts are so many. If Deering had known that those letters had been found, would he be smiling like that? He did know. That was why he was smiling that dark smile. He knew, and he had put Bob up to this. Let the galled jade wince. Jade: J, A, Jade. J, A, Jane. Jade, Jane, Jezebel. The dogs shall eat Jezebel in the portion of Jezreel. Dogs. Dogging his footsteps. The Hound of Heaven with a saucepan lid on his head. Jehovah. JAH. J, A, Jane …

The lights went out.

They had draped a sheet over some chairs to form a little tent. At the door sat Bob, in the dressing-gown and the white beard, but without the saucepan lid. Paul Barnaby, wearing a handkerchief over his head and a short tunic with a sash round the waist, presented him with a frugal meal of two dried figs on a plate. In front of the tent stood a tin bath full of water and surrounded with aspidistras.

A noise of mingled instruments heralded the approach of George, in an Oriental costume of surpassing magnificence and a headdress made of a gilt wastepaper basket. Attended by a train of Oriental followers, he approached Bob, and indicated, with gestures of distress, some livid patches of flour on his face and arms. Bob examined him carefully, clapped him cordially on the shoulder and indicated the tin bath, going through a pantomime of washing. George seemed to be overcome with indignation and contempt. He kicked the bath scornfully and spat vulgarly into the aspidistras. Then, shaking his fist at Bob, he stalked away in high dudgeon in the direction of the piano.

'Hi!' shouted Tony Withers, 'where's your chariot, old man?'

'Shut up!' returned George, disconcerted, 'we can't do that horse business over again.'

Lavinia, modestly attired in a kind of yashmak, now took the stage. Kneeling at George's feet, she gently expostulated with him. The other Oriental followers joined their petitions to hers, and presently his frown relaxed. Returning to the tin bath, and being solemnly supplied with a piece of soap and a loofah, he scrubbed the flour from his face. On observing the effect in a shaving-mirror, he was transported with joy, prostrated himself before Bob and offered him a handsome collection of cushion covers and drawing-room ornaments. These being refused, he went away rejoicing, followed, surreptitiously, by Paul Barnaby. Bob appeared gratified by this result, and was just sitting down to read the *Evening News* in his tent when he observed Paul slinking back through the door with an armful of cushion covers. Overcome with righteous anger he rose to his feet and, dexterously drawing from behind the newspaper a bag of flour, flung it over Paul's face, thus closing the episode.

Markham vaguely heard the applause, but his eyes were fixed on the purple curtains. He knew them so well. They were heavy and swung into thick, rich folds. Jane had adored those curtains. He had always said they were dark and gloomy, but she would hear nothing against them. Nowadays people lived so publicly, behind thin casement cloth and stuff like that; but that old-fashioned damask was made for concealment. Curtains like those kept their secrets forever.

Bice Taylor spoke almost in his ear.

'I don't believe it's either Naaman or Elisha. I think it's Abigail, don't you? The little maid, you know. Not so obvious. It might be J, E, A, something. Jean somebody, or the French Jean.'

J for Jezebel, A for Adam, N for Naaman the leper. J, A, N, Jane, Janitor, January. This was November. Jane died in June.

'What nonsense – Abigail was somebody quite different. It's Gehazi, of course.'

'Gehazi? My dear child – there's no name in four letters beginning JEG or JAG.'

'Yes, there is. There's JAGO.'

'Who's Jago?'

'I don't know. Somebody wrote a book called *John Jago's Ghost*. I do know that.'

'It isn't a book. It's a short story by Wilkie Collins.'

'Oh! is it? I only remember the title.'

'But who was Jago, anyway?'

'I don't know, except that he had a ghost. And what was the point of bringing Gehazi in if it isn't Gehazi?'

'Oh, that's just to make it more difficult.'

Gehazi – Naaman – He went out from before him a leper as white as snow One felt like a leper among all these people who hated one. Leper. See the leopard-dog-thing something at his side, a leer and a lie in every eye. It was so queer that nobody would look at him. They looked round and over him at each other. That was because he was a leper – but they need never know that unless he told them. He had never noticed the pattern on the curtains before, but now the strong light showed it up – damask, damascened like a sword, damn the lot of them. How hot it was, and what a stupid oaf Bob Lester looked, playing childish games. But it was really horrible, the way these people pretended not to know that it was J, A, N, Jane. They did know, really, all the time and were wondering how long he would stick it. Let them wonder! All the same, he must think out what to do when it came to the complete word. J, A, N. Of course, if the last letter wasn't

E … but it was bound to be E. Well, it would be a relief in a way, because then he would know that they knew.

The fourth scene was, for a change, medieval and brief. Betty in white robes, her long hair loosed, oared on the spare-room mattress across the parquet to where Arthur's Court stood grouped by the piano. Bob, simply but effectively armed in corrugated cardboard, weeping fat tears out of a sponge.

'Well, *that's* obvious,' said Mrs Lester. 'The Lady of Shalott. Now, dear me, what can the word be?'

'Oh, *dear* Mrs Lester. Not Shalott. It's Lancelot and Thingummy.'

'Oh, Lancelot, is it?'

'Or, of course, Thingummy.'

'Especially Thingummy,' said Deering.

'Have you guessed it, Tom?'

'Yes, of course. Haven't you?'

'Well, I *think* so, but I'm not absolutely certain.'

'You mustn't say until the end.'

'No, all right.'

Oh, yes, thought Markham. Deering would have guessed it, of course. Lancelot and Elaine. Elaine the lovable. Jane, Elaine. J, A, N, E, Jane. But it was all wrong, because Elaine was pure and faithful and died of love. Died. That was the point. Elaine was dead. Jane was dead. Jane, Elaine as Jane had lain.

He fixed his eyes on the damask curtains. There was one point where they did not quite meet, and the light from the stage showed through. Somebody called 'Are you ready?' and turned off the switch on the side of the spectators.

Markham could not see them any longer, but he could hear them breathing and rustling about him, packed close like wolves, pressing in upon him. The point of light still shone between the curtains. It grew larger, and glowed more intensely, yet as though from an enormous distance.

Then, very slowly this time, and in absolute silence, the curtains parted. The whole word at last.

They had done a wonderful piece of staging this time. He recognised every object, though the blaze of the electric globe had been somehow subdued. There was the bed and the dressing-table and the wardrobe with its tall glass door, and the low casement on the right. It was hot, and the scent of the syringa – philadelphus, the books said, but Jane called it syringa – came billowing in from the garden in thick puffs. The girl on the bed was asleep. Her face was hidden, turned to the wall. Dying people always turned to the wall. Too bad to have to die in June, with the scent of the syringa coming in through the window and the nightingale singing so loudly. Did they do that with a bird-whistle, or was it a gramophone record?

Somebody was moving in the shadows. He had opened the door very gently. There was a glass of lemonade on the table by the bed. It chinked against the bottle as he picked it up, but the girl did not move. He walked right forward till he stood directly beneath the light. His head was bent down as he shot the white powder into the glass and stirred it with a spoon. He went back to the bedside, walking like Agag, delicately. A, G, A, G, Adam and Gehazi. Jezebel, Adam, Naaman, Elaine, J, A, N, E. He touched the girl on the shoulder and she stirred a little. He put one arm behind her shoulders and held the glass to her lips. It clinked again as he set it down empty. Then he kissed her. He went out, shutting the door.

He had never known such silence. He could not even hear the wolfpack breathing. He was alone in the room with the girl who lay on the bed. And now she was moving. The sheet slipped from her shoulders to her breast, from her breast to her waist. She was rising to her knees, lifting herself up to face him over the footboard of the bed – gold hair, sweat-streaked forehead, eyes dark with fear and pain, black hollow of the mouth, and the glittering line of white teeth in the fallen jaw.

JANE!

Had he cried out; or had they? The room was full of light and noise, but his voice rose above it.

'Jane, Jezebel! I killed her. I poisoned her. Jane, jade, Jezebel. The doctor never knew, but she knew, and he knew, and now you all know. Get out! damn you! curse you! Let me go!'

Chairs were falling, people were shouting, clutching at him. He smashed a fist into a silly, gaping face. He was on the balcony. He was fighting for the balustrade. The lights on the Surrey side were like tall Japanese lanterns. He was over. The black water leapt to meet him. Cataracts, roaring.

It had all happened so quickly that the actors knew nothing about it. As Tom Deering pulled off his coat to dive after Markham and Mrs Lester rushed to telephone the river police, George's voice announced 'The Whole Word', and the curtains were flung open to display the tent of JAEL.

Credits

'The Snapdragon and the CID' by Margery Allingham reprinted by permission of Peters Fraser & Dunlop (*www.petersfraserdunlop.com*) on behalf of the estate of Margery Allingham

'Let Nothing You Dismay!' by Ellis Peters, reprinted by permission of United Agents

'Tooth of the Lion' by Edmund Crispin, reprinted by permission of Peters Fraser & Dunlop (*www.petersfraserdunlop.com*) on behalf of the estate of Edmund Crispin

'Rumpole and the Spirit of Christmas' from *Rumpole at Christmas* by John Mortimer (Penguin Books, 2009). Copyright © Advanpress Ltd, 2009

'The Assassins Club' by Nicholas Blake, reprinted by permission of Peters Fraser & Dunlop (*www.petersfraserdunlop.com*) on behalf of the estate of Nicholas Blake